# Clydesdale
## HAS A MIDSUMMER'S NIGHTMARE

First Edition

Published by The Nazca Plains Corporation
Las Vegas, Nevada
2011

ISBN: 978-1-61098-188-0
Ebook: 978-1-61098-189-7

Published by

The Nazca Plains Corporation ®
4640 Paradise Rd, Suite 141
Las Vegas NV 89109-8000

PUBLISHER'S NOTE
*Clydesdale Has a Midsummer's Nightmare* is a work of fiction created wholly by *Bob Archman*'s imagination. All characters are fictional and any resemblance to any persons living or deceased is purely by accident. No portion of this book reflects any real person or events.

Male Cover Photo, Christopher Howey
Outdoor Cover Photo, Yuryz

Art Director, Blake Stephens

# Clydesdale
## HAS A MIDSUMMER'S NIGHTMARE

First Edition

Published by The Nazca Plains Corporation
Las Vegas, Nevada
2011

# Prelude

## *Clydesdale meets some Elves*

It was Christmas Eve and I was in LAX. Things weren't looking good. There was a snowstorm in Denver and that backed up all planes going east. I was heading for Richmond, but by the particular logic of modern air schedule planning there wasn't much hope I would make it.

At noon there seemed to be a chance I could make it. There was a flight to Vancouver, then on to Toronto, then to Washington. It would be possible to get south from there. I was working with a young ticket agent and she was trying her best to make the connections. It was still possible at five. Suddenly I had a ticket. When I got to the check in, I was next to a young girl and her even younger brother. They were on standby and only one ticket was available for the two of them.

The girl was frantic, the boy was trying to be brave and not cry. I spoke with the airline attendant and let them take my seat. It would be nice to get home for Christmas, but I'm a middle-aged man, and it was no big deal.

I called my friend in Richmond on the cell phone and told them of my problem. As it turned out, he wasn't feeling well and was more than willing to celebrate Christmas a day or two later. All was well. My ticket agent was still giving it a try, but she was hoping to get home to her children, so I told her not to worry. I'd wait for the next day.

The airline had hired a Santa and two elves to cheer up the customers and ease the stress of waiting. They had been trying to help the kids when I came to their rescue. They went off to help others and I forgot about my brief meeting with them.

I decided to give up on getting east. When I tried to get a hotel room, I found out all the hotels nearby were filled to capacity. I decided to stay in the airport for the night. My chances were better at getting an early flight out the next morning that way.

I was in the men's room taking a leak when I heard a voice saying, "That's one hell of a piece of meat! Your momma must have been fucked by a donkey." There was no one there. I looked down and saw one of the elves.

I smiled, "I won't ask who fucked your momma."

The elf laughed. "I see you're smarter than you look as well as being hung like Trigger," he said. "You're the guy who helped those kids aren't you? It was a nice thing to do."

"Well, there ain't that many toys under my tree anymore," I remarked. The elf was still looking at my cock. I'm uncut and meaty and you can tell that even when I'm soft. He looked interested. I guessed my elf was a cock fancier. I zipped up.

"Did you get a flight, or a hotel room?" he asked as we left the rest room and went to a quiet part of the lobby. By now, the news of the Denver storm was generally known and the crowd had diminished.

"Neither," I replied, "But to tell you the truth, I've slept in a lot of places much worse than an airport lobby."

"I've got a room in the Airport Hilton across the way," he said. "I'm sharing it with my pal Rudy, but we're small. There's room for you."

"I thought you'd be busy delivering toys with Santa," I said. I sat in one of the waiting room chairs. Sitting I could look at him more closely. He was solid looking and I would guess he was in his forties. He had a luxuriant blond beard and twinkling blue eyes. He appeared to be muscular and well-proportioned other than his short legs.

"My name's David, by the way," he said.

"Clydesdale is the name here."

He looked at me for a second or two. "A horse-hung Clydesdale? Am I right?"

"You guessed it," I replied. "I appreciate the offer, but..."

"I was thinking of you being my toy for the night," David said. "I was kind of hoping you were the playful type. You've got a lot to play with."

"I guess you're the kind of guy we call open minded, back east," I said.

"For you, everything's open," he said. David climbed up on the sat next to me and whispered in my ear, "Are you a top?"

"I sure am, but..."

"Don't worry about that," he said. "In spite of my size, I'm a big boy. You aren't exactly basketball player material. You can be the tallest guy in the room for once."

"That's an offer I can't refuse," I said.

"You stay here while I tell Rudy," David said as he scampered away.

I wondered if he would return. Many gay men have bigger eyes than ass holes. It's fun to look at a big cock, but when it comes to getting up close and personal with one, it's different. Ten minutes later, he returned. "I thought you had lost interest," I said.

"Not at all," David replied. "There is a little fly in the ointment though. Rudy has invited some friends over tonight."

"You mean I'm not going to be the tallest man in the room now?"

"No, they're all little people," he replied. He climbed onto the seat again. "It's going to be a sex party. I didn't know if you'd be interested," he whispered.

"How many guys?"

"Six, maybe eight."

"What makes you think I'd like to have sex with eight guys I've never even met?" I asked. David looked crest fallen. "Actually, it sounds pretty good to me. Are they all good sports?"

He perked up. "Rudy knows them, not me. He says they're lots of fun."

Fifteen minutes later, we took a taxi to the hotel. Rudy was a black-haired version of David. Both men were cheerful and seemed affable. At the hotel, they ordered food from room service. It was a surprisingly good steak dinner. We talked as we ate and I got to know the two men. I had no experience with dwarfs and didn't know what to expect.

They were two successful actors. Rudy was a native of Hollywood and he tended to play wise old dwarfs in fantasy movies. His beard was real and the role didn't seem to be a stretch for him. David was from Reno and he was more of a circus performer. He was athletic and a natural gymnast-acrobat. This wasn't their usual gig. They were substituting for friends who had families.

They had been lovers at one time and were still friends. David had come to LA to spend the holiday with Rudy and was just helping out. Apparently, the party was a surprise for David. David had moved to Reno to take care of his elderly mother. She was visiting a sister for the holiday. He didn't get out much and Rudy wanted to get a year or so of sex into one night. I figured it would have to be one hell of a party to do that, but it was a nice gesture.

Room service picked up the dinner trays. Rudy had two cases of beer on the balcony. It wasn't cold but it was cool by the standards of Southern California. David went off to get some lubricant from a nearby adult "novelty" store.

"David says you're hung like Trigger," Rudy said after David left. "He's a bit of a size queen."

"You're not?"

"Not really," Rudy admitted, "but I could be converted. David was so excited, I couldn't say no."

"I'm into fun, not pain. I don't put in anywhere it's not wanted," I explained. "I tend to go with the flow. I like to top, but I've had a good time on the bottom too. To tell you the truth if someone could find a new way to get off, I'd be willing to try it."

"You're a man after my own heart," Rudy said. He was silent. "I'm ready to get this party underway. Want to get naked?"

I said, "Sure." I began to strip. Rudy undressed too.

"Damn, you're a hairy one," he said. "I thought I was hairy, but you take the cake."

"Is that a problem?"

"Not for me," he said. By then I had dropped my pants. I'm not into strip teases, so I dropped my Jockeys too. "Shit, David was right. What in hell do you do with that thing?"

I smiled. "I do the usual things," I replied. "The question is what you want to do with it."

"I can think of a lot of things," he said. "Have you noticed I'm at just the right height to suck without bending over?" Rudy had his shirt off, exposing his hairy chest and big, pink nipples. He hesitated before taking off his pants. He finally dropped his pants. He had a pair of ping-pong ball sized nuts and a knob the same size wrapped in a thick foreskin.

"Jump up on the bed and let me look," I said. He did as I asked. I then took his cock into my mouth and worked my tongue into his foreskin. I licked his cock head. There was a good store of precum in there and a fresh supply oozing as I sucked.

"I think we're going to get along well," he said. Someone knocked at the door.

"Company's here," Rudy said.

"I hope I'm not over dressed," I said.

"I think you're going to be a hit," he said. Rudy opened the door and three little people entered. One man was dressed in a camel hair sports coat, looked at me and said, "That isn't David is it?"

"Look at that cock!" another one exclaimed. This man was a muscleman who had the physique of a diminutive Steve Reeves, or of Arnold.

"Boys, this is Clydesdale," Rudy said. "He's a stranded traveler David found in the airport."

"What is it about him David found appealing?" the muscleman asked as he looked at my cock. I was half hard and looking good.

"I think I'm supposed to be the entertainment," I said. "I'm in place of the pony or the clown."

The third man in the group took off his clothes, came over to me, and started to suck.

"Wally has the right idea," Rudy said. A minute or two later we were all naked and rolling around on the bed. The man in the camel hair coat was Doc, a child psychologist; the muscleman was Trevor who was a nationally known weightlifter. Wally was a computer programmer.

About ten minutes later David arrived with two men. They were twins, Don and Dan. I felt for the first and only time in my life like Gulliver. All of us were naked and erect. I didn't know much about little people, but it was clear to me the seven dwarfs were different. The Twins and Trevor were miniature people, well portioned. Rudy, David and Wally had full size trunks and small legs. Doc was had small legs and hands. David and the twins were well hung. The others had nice equipment at a small scale. Doc had oversized equipment. His short legs made his cock and low hangers look huge.

"Oh shit," Doc said. "We have seven Dwarfs in this room!" We all burst out laughing.

"Does that make me Snow White?" I asked. There was more laughter.

"If you're Snow White there is a serious malfunction in the mirror!" Wally said.

"I'll play Snow White if you want me too, but the Mae West quote, "I use to be snow white, but I drifted," may be more appropriate," I added to the conversation.

"Most of us know each other," Doc said. "Would you be offended if I asked you what's your poison? We're only together for one night so we might as well find out what you want."

"Doc is the direct type," Rudy said.

"I'm direct too," I said, "I'm 56 years old now and I can truthfully say there nothing that involves a cock and an asshole I don't like. Maybe I've been lucky, but I liked man sex the first time I tried it, and it just gets better. I top. I bottom. I suck. I'm an old dog, but I can learn new tricks."

"You've never had sex with a dwarf before?" Doc asked.

"Nope, but where there's a will, there's a way," I replied. "I don't know what will fit where, but there are some easy ways to find out. I'm game if you're game." It turned out they were all game.

Somehow, they turned my body into a playground. David wanted to sit on my cock. Doc wanted to fuck me. They put a pillow under my ass, raising it so he could get his organ in my ass as David sat back on my cock.

Doc was what I would call a hard but fair fucker. His cock blew up like a balloon, it was thick, but tapered as it reached his body. The taper formed a natural cock ring. He stayed hard and didn't get tired of thrusting. The cock was a good fit for my ass. He lubricated his cock well, but it took some effort to get it past my sphincter. Once it was in, it felt good and got better the longer he fucked me.

As Doc fucked me, David was impaling himself on my cock. This took lots of lube and lots of encouragement from the other men. They were a supportive group squirting lube on my cock, or in his hole as necessary. When I got half of it in, he almost gave up. He sat up and rested. Wally squirted fresh lube in his ass, and he tried again.

As he sat back a second time, Rudy produced a fresh bottle of poppers. David took a deep snort. This seemed to do the trick. When David fully impaled himself, Doc shot off. I could feel him shiver and shake as he ejaculated. He pulled out. By that time, David was use to my cock. I could feel him relaxing and letting my cock slip deeper into his body.

I know many bottoms and I sensed David wanted to be fucked, not just sit with my cock nine inches in his ass. "Are you ready for a little doggie style action?" I asked. David nodded. He got off my cock. I got two pillows and bent him over them. After adding lubricant to my cock, I slid in deep. Bending over him, I held him tight as I made thrusting motions with my hips.

I had to slow down a few times because he couldn't breathe, but he loved it. He had a very muscular ass, so he stayed tight, even though his rectum was velvety soft. As I fucked him, I spread my legs wider. Someone started playing with my ass.

I looked back and saw it was the twins. They were working a few fingers into my hole. They had small hands and it was exciting. Something much bigger started penetrating my ass. I was puzzled since Doc had the biggest cock in the group and he had already fucked me. I felt a sharp pain, and then the object slipped in deep. It was huge.

"What in hell is that?" I asked.

"It's Trevor's fist and half his arm," Donald said.

"Oh shit."

"Do you want us to stop?" Trevor asked.

"It's okay. Just take it easy," I said. David began to moan. I had him firmly under control and I could feel cum shooting. His ass contracted with every ejaculation. I pulled out. Trevor pulled out too. I felt like a wet dishrag.

"Have you ever been fisted before?" Trevor asked.

"Nope. This is a first," I said.

"Are you okay?"

"Yep. You did it well," I replied.

Trevor was silent. "Do you think you could let me do it again?" he asked. "It was really exciting."

"It's too much," Doc said. "Clydesdale has been a really good sport. We shouldn't take advantage of him." David had snuggled up to me, as had the twins. I was feeling mellow and relaxed.

"If you let me catch my breath, I'll do it again," I said. "I'm kind of confused now. I'm not sure what I was feeling."

We all had a beer or two and calmed down. I drank as someone sucked my cock. I would lick a cock or two between swigs. Wally was getting it on with one of the twins and Rudy bent over the bed, sipping beer as Doc fucked him. It was a nice relaxing period of casual sex between friends.

The phone rang. David answered it. H spoke for a while and then pressed the hold button. "It's Santa. He'd like to come over. He just got off duty. Is it okay with you guys?"

"I take it he's with the program?" Doc asked.

"He's a 100% sex pig," Rudy answered. "A nice guy too."

"Well, tell him what we are doing and make sure he knows what he's getting into," Doc said.

"Well Santa, how does a Christmas Eve orgy sound to you?" David asked. We could hear Santa saying "Hot Damn" in the room. They told him to come over. Fifteen minutes later Santa was at the door. He entered the room, looked around at the naked men and stripped with incredible speed. He was heavily padded and had been sweating like a pig. He took a shower and joined us on the bed.

Santa was a good 6'3" and was well above 240 pounds, most of it muscles. He was bald with a massive and flamboyant white beard. His body was furry too. He was a classic polar bear. He had a meaty, uncut cock. Santa's real name was Frederic and he was a noted Shakespearean actor. He played Santa when he was between plays. David and Rudy never used his real name just in case they made a slip in public.

It was clear he had played with David and Rudy. The other men were new to him, but Santa wasn't the shy type.

While Santa met the standards of being a jolly old elf, he was also a natural leader of men. In some ways, he was as far from the traditional vision of a handsome man as you could be. He wasn't slim. He wasn't young. He didn't have prefect hair. He was a fuzzy hairball of a man.

Santa was cheerful and happy, full of enthusiasm and full of life. He was attractive and had a magnetic personality, a natural leader of men.

You wanted to be near him and wanted to please him. You sensed he would give more than he got. He would say, "Let's try this," and everyone would try it.

His cock was of a more reasonable size than mine was. Wrapped in foreskin, it looked huge, but when he was erect, it consisted of a large mushroom on a thin shaft. Rudy was the first to sit on Santa's love pole. It was hard getting the head past Rudy's sphincter, but once it was it, it was pure prostate pleasure.

Later Santa was on his hands and knees sucking both of the twins as Wally fucked him. That left me with Doc, Trevor, Rudy and David. We formed a happy band. I sucked Doc while the other three took turns fucking me.

Being fucked by the small men was anatomically difficult. It turned out Santa was into anal big time. I've always been into cocks. Santa loved ass holes. He got me on my back, then pushed my legs over my chest and had me hook them with my arms. This pretzel position left my asshole wide open and easily accessible. It was easy for the dwarfs to fuck me.

I'm not a natural bottom, but I had fun. You could say I'm a social bottom the way some people are social drinkers. It was more recreational than fucking. Every single one of them fucked me, and several came back for seconds. It was stimulating, fun and relaxing as the elves' cocks opened me up.

I had never played the bottom slut before, but I enjoyed it. While I don't want to sound too much like Mother Theresa, but I enjoyed watching the men enjoy themselves in my ass. Santa took advantage of my open ass a few times too.

Most of this was just simply old-fashioned fun, but several times, it got more intense. Trevor, the bodybuilder, was a handsome man and I am about as unhandsome a man can be. Trevor wasn't really interested in fucking me, but a hot ass is a hot ass, and he took his turn. He had a long, quite thin cock that unexpectedly hit just the right place in my ass.

From time to time, I've been accused of letting my cock do my thinking for me. That's true some times, but I'm not the only one. Trevor was shocked to discover, while he had no interest in me, his cock was in love. Where the brain in your cock leads your real brain often follows. Trevor and I had an incredibly hot session. When his cock head rammed my prostate, my sphincter closed tight, grabbing his cock in a vice like grip. I not that muscular, but I have a sphincter of steel. When I grabbed his cock, he tried to pull out. He got to the point when only his cock head was still in my ass and reconsidered. He rammed me again.

For the next ten minutes we discovered there was nothing his cock could do, or my ass could do that was not entirely satisfactory to both of us. Pleasure turned into passion. We were like crazed dogs in heat.

We were also inspirational, and soon everyone was going at it. We came damn close to having a joint orgasm. Overall, it was a very satisfactory interlude. Trevor shot off in my ass then rolled on my sperm covered body, like a dog who found a dead fish. I had shot off a good load and several of the other guys added their seed to the brew. Trevor was coated in the stuff and he worked the man jiz into my hairy chest.

I went to take a shower with Trevor and Doc. Dried cum is difficult to get off. Sometimes sex with strangers can be good, and this was one of these times. It was sex, pure and unadulterated. We were all after fun and nothing more.

Santa joined us after a few minutes. He hugged me and then we kissed. Doc was nursing my cock and Trevor was sucking Santa. I had just shot off, but I was still excited. "The boys tell me you played the hand puppet earlier tonight, "Santa said. "I'd like to see that. I've never seen a man being fisted. Who did it?"

"Trevor did, but there are several who'd like to try it," Doc said.

"Are you still a good sport, Clydesdale?" Santa asked.

"I guess I am," I said. Trevor stopped sucking him and was at Santa's rear. "And you?" I asked. Santa nodded. We got out of the shower, dried off and got on the bed. Apparently, Santa and the elves had been talking while I was in the shower. The small men were looking at Santa and they broke into smiles when they saw Santa smiling. I hate to think they knew me better than I did, but they seemed to think I'd be agreeable.

Santa told me if I could do it, he'd try it next. It's embarrassing to admit it, but I hadn't focused on the men's arms. I had noticed their legs and of course as a card-carrying gay man, their cocks, but not their arms.

I was back on the bed with my legs spread eagled. As I said, Santa was into ass holes and he was front row and center giving advice to the small men on how to get into my ass.

"Are you sure you've never done this before?" I asked.

"Yes, but I have seen it in a movie or two," Santa said. "I've talked to some men who have done it."

"Do they like it?" Doc asked.

"That's what interests me," Santa said. "They do it, but they seem to be cagy about what they're feeling. I'd like to know. You've got a good hole." He was fingering my hole and had a tube of lubricant ready. I was going to complain, but he had a finger on each side of my prostate. He gently squeezed the tender organ. I could hardly talk. The pleasure was that intense. Santa knew his way around an ass.

"Be careful, Wally. It's really delicate in there," Doc said. I glanced over and saw Wally lubricating his hand and forearm. "Take your time and take it easy."

Santa took his fingers out of my hole and Wally came up. His hand was small. He started with one finger toying with my hole. A second and a third finger followed shortly.

"Relax Clydesdale, you're with friends," Doc said. Wally was pushing harder now and stretching my ass. "Take a sniff!" Santa ordered. He held a bottle of poppers to my nose. Wally pushed as I inhaled. It hurt when his hand penetrated the sphincter but it was it wasn't bad.

"Damn, it's into the wrist," Rudy whispered. "Push deeper!"

"Hold up!" Doc ordered. "Are you okay, Clydesdale?" I nodded. "Form your hand into a fist, Wally. Make sure your finger nails are in the fist. You don't want to scrape anything." Doc said. "Move it around in there and see what happens."

It didn't take long for Wally to find my prostate. I moaned. Rudy gave me another snort of the poppers and Wally pushed deeper. Eventually, Wally was into my ass up to his elbow. I've taken some big cocks, but the biggest cock can't do anything but thrust. Having a clenched hand moving in my ass was an all-new experience. Sexually I think the pressure on my prostate was most striking.

Wally was careful. I was very tense, uneasy and excited. I had no idea what to do. It was uncomfortable to be without any control. Wally was in charge. Doc must have sensed my concern. "You can relax," he said. "I know these boys. You're in good hands." The pun was accidental. "Pull out slowly, Wally. Clydesdale needs a rest."

Wally did as Doc said. The stress vanished, as did the excitement. Santa got on the bed next to me. He spread his legs wide. "It's my turn now," Santa said. "I'd like to give it a try."

"I'm ready!" the twins said in unison. Everyone laughed. They double-teamed Santa. Doc again gave instructions and made sure Santa was okay. As far as I could tell, there wasn't a sadistic or masochistic bone in anyone's body.

Santa was more of a bottom than I was. He really enjoyed the twins. They alternated penetrations. Dan and Don operated as a couple, and when Dan went into his wrist, the next time Don would go in two inches deeper. They stopped at the elbow. Santa was in heaven.

Once in deep, Dan would rotate his fist, massaging the insides of Santa's ass. It sounds crude when you describe it, but the twins were gentle and almost delicate in their approach to sex. It was more as if they were massaging Santa's privates than fist fucking him. It was almost midnight by now and I was tired. I was on the bed watching Santa twitching and the next thing I knew it was seven thirty in the morning.

I climbed out of bed and over the sleeping bodies and got to the bath. After relieving myself, I took a shower. When I got out, Doc was waiting for me.

"How are you doing?" he asked. "I'm afraid we used and abused you last night."

"Used, but not abused," I replied. "I've never been too clear on who uses whom in sex. Maybe when brides were sold to husbands there was a problem. Sex for me is more of a mutual admiration society. It's a 50-50 proposition."

"That's a healthy approach to sex," Doc said, "but it wasn't 50-50 last night."

"I like for it to average out to 50-50," I said, smiling. "It's not much fun if you're keeping score all the time."

"I can't tell you how turned on I was while watching Wally's arm vanish in your ass," Doc said. "That you were uneasy about it excited me too."

"Why is that?"

"When you're my size, it's hard to make a fully grown man squirm," Doc said. "Mostly people laugh at us. The idea of dwarfs having sex is more comic than sexual."

"Well, no one tried to recruit me for the basketball team when I was a kid," I said. "When I'm naked, I'm a magnet for size queens, but you can't walk around town with your cock dragging on the ground all the time. I'm not a stud magnet."

Doc commented, "I'm a bit of a size queen myself, but your cock isn't an option. It's about twice the length and three times the diameter of anything I've taken." He paused. "I was really turned on last night."

I looked at Doc and saw he had tube of lube with him. I realized what he wanted. His head was at crotch height. He began kissing my cock. He didn't suck it. He made love to it. He had a mustache and beard that tickled.

"You fucked me two or three times yesterday," I said. "That wasn't enough?"

"You're a polite guy, Clydesdale," Doc said as he worked his tongue into my foreskin. "I'd like to ring your chimes, big time."

"What kind of a counselor are you?"

"I'm a psychiatrist," Doc replied. "I work regularly with sexual dysfunction."

"You think that's my problem?"

"Quite the opposite," he replied. "You seem like an open book. As far as I can tell, you're normal."

"Other than having the sex drive of a baboon?"

Doc smiled. "There is that. You are sexually generous, and you aren't a predator. Sex comes to you. You're masculine, but you're not driven." Doc said. "When you've got the right tool, you don't need the attitude." I shifted my stance a little wider. Doc's hand was at my ass immediately.

"You also don't associate pain with sex and you don't need pain to get off," Doc continued. "The pain-sex link can be dangerous." David entered the room and climbed up on the toilet seat, he had a box of ampoules. Doc had worked everything out before. He had pure amyl nitrate waiting for me.

By now doc had his fingers in my ass and was pumping. "I was wondering if one of your interests as a doctor was sexual anatomy?" I asked.

"You guessed it," Doc said. "I'm interested in the connection between your sex organ and your brain. David, give him a snort." David broke the ampoule in its cloth sheath and held it to my nose. I inhaled. A second later, I was on the way to the moon, and Doc's hand was in my ass.

"Give me one, David," Doc ordered. He sniffed the ampoule and went after my cock. As he sucked it, his arm went in deep. If I had more sense, I'd have been worried. Poppers can make you overly enthusiastic and that I didn't need in a man whose arm was up my ass.

There wasn't a problem. Doc had it all worked out. He knew where he wanted to go and what he wanted to do. As far as I could tell, he did it all. David surprised me when he got on Doc's shoulders. He had a tube of lube that he used on my cock. David broke open another ampoule, took a deep breath and gave it to me.

David then put his arms around my neck and his legs around my waist. Doc had his arm up my ass, but his other hand held my cock still, so David could impale himself again. He wiggled his ass as he took my entire organ. Doc was working my ass as my cock worked David's hole.

"You're going to shoot!" Doc cried. He was right. My orgasm was so strong, I half expected to see my cream shooting from David's mouth. I was twitching and jerking with each ejaculation. With each jerk, I went deeper into David's ass. Doc pulled out a little, which was good. Too much of a good thing can be a problem. David shot off too. I was dizzy for a little while, but was able to help David off my cock. Doc watched, with a big smile on his face. I saw his cock was rock hard, so I lifted him up onto the toilet seat, fell to my knees and sucked him. The second my tongue touched his cock head he blew.

"Ho, Ho, Ho," A jolly old Elf said from the door. "I see you boys found your presents!" Santa was holding Rudy, supporting him by his arms and his cock. The best toys are the simplest ones, and attached to your body.

# Part I

*The Play*

It had been a quiet period at my office. We had things under control. Most of our clients were happy and crime had taken a holiday. One afternoon I got a call from Santa. Several years earlier, I had spent a Christmas with Santa and his elves. There had been a storm and airports were closed. Santa and his elves asked me to their room and we had screwed our way through the holiday. Santa was a well-known Shakespearean actor who specialized in playing Falstaff and other comic roles.

He was in Richmond for a play. "Clydesdale, we've got a problem," he said. "I think something bad is going on here."

"Tell me more," I said.

"I'm with the Duke of Richmond's Company. It's a new Shakespearean troop here. We're doing the second play of our first season. Did you read about Lady Macbeth?" I had. It had been a mostly female cast reworking of Macbeth. They set the play on a Scottish island inhabited by Amazon warriors. It had been daring and original. "I'm here playing Bottom in a Midsummer Night's Dream. It's going to be an actual period production with Elizabethan costumes and an all-male cast. Young men will be playing the female roles. David and Rudy are here playing the fairies. They're all going to be played by dwarfs. Don and David are here too."

"What is the problem?"

"Poison pen letters. Actually they are more like threats," he said.

"Are they that bad?"

"There is something very wrong about them. It may be a stalker; maybe it's an obsessed fan. They are ugly."

"Is there anyone in the play who is famous enough to have a stalker?" I asked.

"Not even close. That's the problem. It makes no sense at all," Santa said. "I have a bad feeling about it. Could you look into it?"

I said I'd help.

The next day I went to an old theater on Broad Street that was the rehearsal hall for the company. Santa greeted me. It was mostly a young company. Santa was the daddy. I met the director, Charlie Smith; he was 35 or so and went to the office. They had several of the letters. Poison pen letters are usually poorly written with multiple grammatical errors and spelling problems. These were carefully written and seemed to indicate intimate knowledge of the victim's lives.

"I think we have a voyeur," I said. "Have there been any incidents?"

"A tire was slashed," Charlie said. "My partner had a problem with his car breaks. One of our actors was followed. Nothing happened, but he was scared."

"I can get some men to watch the area around the theater," I said.

"I think we need someone inside," Santa said.

"There's no question someone on the inside is involved," Charlie said. "I don't know if it's a spy, or the letter writer himself."

"I have a role for you to play in the production, Clydesdale," Santa said. "Are you familiar with a Midsummer Night's Dream?"

"I only know the name," I said

"There is a play within the play. It's a love story and a fantasy about fairies and woodland sprites, but there are comic interludes featuring rude mechanics putting on a play," Santa said.

"Are you thinking no one could be more rustic than me?"

Santa smiled. "Well the thought did occur to me. The roles are small except for mine. I am Bottom the ultimate buffoon. The other roles are minor and it would give you a good excuse for being here."

"Do I have any lines?"

"Very few," Charlie said. "I was thinking about you playing Tom Snout, a wall."

"A wall?"

"It's a long story,"

"Does it make any sense?"

"Technically no," Charlie said.  "It's a romp.  That why Frederic is here.  It takes a good actor to make it work."

"Frederic? Oh, you mean Santa." I said.  It was easy to forget Santa was Frederic DeVille, a well-known actor who pinch hit as Santa if he wasn't working on a play at Christmas.

"If you were to call me Fred rather than Santa it would be nice, Clydesdale."

"Maybe you should call me Will.  Someone might get the connection to my security firm," I said.

I joined the Duke of Richmond's Players.  They gave me a movie to watch.  That would be an easier way to get into the play than reading it.  I got to like it after the second time.  It was three stories that touched accidentally.  Bottom was funny and over the top.  I could see how it would be fun if it were well acted.

The next day I went to rehearsal.  In the morning, I went over each of the actors' resumes and photos.  About half of the company had gone to a local university.  Another quarter lived in Richmond, but had been trained elsewhere.  The remainder of the cast members were from outside.  Many of these were the dwarfs who were playing the fairies.

Since so much of the cast attended the same local university, I would do some checking on that.  I had some connections there.  Later when I met the actors, I didn't recognize many of them from their headshots.  They all had a good photographer.

There may have been a few straight men in the group, but there weren't many.  There was a full range of gay types from leather punks to flaming queens.  The dwarfs added an element of fantasy.  David and Rudy were there with several younger dwarfs.  They had been Santa's elves when I last saw them.

Charlie introduced me as a new cast member playing the role of the roughcast wall. I said a few words, and the cast seemed to think I was in character as a rustic buffoon in my street clothes. So far so good. I knew the older man playing Theseus, the Duke of Athens, but he gave no indication he knew me. He was John Smithers and was the morning weatherman on Channel 3. He had received one of the letters, so he must have known why I was there.

They did a read through of the first act. All I had to do was to read my lines and act stupid. That I did admirably. After the reading, John came to me and asked if I'd like a cup of coffee. I said sure, so we went to his apartment. It was a few blocks away in a loft building. The young man playing his future wife in the play came with us; his name was Lance.

The apartment was new and well decorated. He got the model apartment when they sold out the building, complete with furnishings. John had a cute Cocker Spaniel named Anchorman and was affable. John was one of those television personalities who went to all the local events and was well known and well liked. He was also one of those men who were more photogenic than handsome.

"I take it you are looking into the problem?" he said.

"Yes. I'm not sure if it is a nasty prank, just someone with really bad attitude or something worse," I said.

"Someone must think it's bad if you're involved?"

"It's still more bad vibes than fact," I said.

"Well someone followed me," Lance said. "I live next to the campus." Lance was in his early 20s and blandly good looking.

"Did you see anything?"

"I caught a glimpse of a man in a long coat," he said. "It was a warm night and the coat was unnecessary."

"You're sure it was a man?"

"Yes. His walk and stance were masculine. I've played female roles and seen women playing men. This was a man," he explained. John sat next to Lance and had his arm around his shoulders. I had met John at a gay party. I had always assumed his sexual preference was why he was still only the morning weatherman.

"Do you have any problems with former friends?" I asked.

"Lovers you mean?" Lance asked. "Not that I am aware at. I tend to be faithful as Anchorman here. They leave me, not the other way around."

"Are you two a couple?" I asked.

Both men laughed. "I think it would be more correct to say we are recreational outlets," John said, "We are plain old friends with benefits."

I smiled. "That can be good too." I had the feeling they had a recreational activity planned after I left.

John was a mind reader. "Would you like to join us for some fun?" he asked. "I'm a bottom and have been trying to develop Lance's top side. He is a natural bottom." I must have looked a little uneasy. "By the way, Lance is a size queen." The three of us adjourned to the bedroom.

Lance was nice enough to be fully erect by the time we had stripped. He had a thin lollipop style cock. John looked good naked. He was well tanned and in good shape. He had shaved his body hair, but it was growing back in an even layer. His cock was shaped like a stumpy butt plug. That John was a bottom was an understatement. As soon as he was naked, he got on the edge of the bed, hooked his legs with his arms and opened his ass wide.

A second or two later Lance's cock head was in John's ass. Lance looked at me with fear and trepidation as I stripped. I think I was a lot more hairy than his usual playmates. When he saw my cock, fear turned to lust. I got on the bed behind John and held his legs open for Lance. My balls dangled in John's face. John licked them, and then he got turned on and we went at it. He shot off easily.

Lance took his time pulling out. My balls were still in John's mouth but I was nice and hard. "It's going to take a lot of lube to get that in me," Lance said.

"Are you getting cold feet?"

Lance smiled. "No, just thinking aloud."

"I take my time, but there's a point of no return," I said. Lance had been slowly stroking his cock as we talked. Suddenly warm stuff began to splatter on my body. He had popped. Lance was as surprised as I was. I asked if I could get a rain check; he readily agreed. I went home.

That evening, I got a call from David. He and the other dwarfs were in an apartment a few blocks from my place. He asked if I could get come by and renew our old acquaintance. I said sure and I walked over.

They were staying in an old Art Deco style apartment house on Grove Avenue. Apparently, the theater company maintained an apartment there for visiting actors. David and his friend, Rudy, were very masculine, bearded men. David was blond and blue eyed, his beard was more luxuriant than I remembered. David had a black beard. David was playing Puck; he had been a gymnast and was in good shape. Rudy was going to Oberon, the fairy king. Don and Dan were Cowslip and Peasebottom.

I didn't know two younger men. Samuel was perhaps 22. He was blond and looked younger than his years. He was to play Titania the queen of the fairies. Tommy was to play Cobweb one of the lesser fairies.

The third floor apartment was nice and well furnished. It was hot. The men were in varied states of undress. When David answered to the door, he whispered, "We're all horny as hell. Is that a problem?" The answer was definitely no. I stripped and got to know the men sexually before I really met them. There was a comical discussion as to exactly what they could do with my cock. Tommy and Samuel agreed it was pretty, but over scaled.

It was fun. Sex with a dwarf is a novelty, and they knew some men did it just to say they did it with a dwarf. I had the same problem with my cock. Some men just wanted to say they could take a cock as big as mine.

I got on the bed and they crawled all over me. David fucked me as Samuel and Rudy jointly sucked my cock. I sucked Tommy. Tommy had a comparatively small cock, but full sized balls. He leaked precum from the second my lips touched his cock. It was a taste treat.

Samuel was effeminate and badly wanted his manhole opened by a big one. He sat on my cock, using it as a stool. David and Rudy supplied lubricant and were into poppers. Sam snorted some poppers. His ass opened and four or five inches of my meat popped into his ass. He sat there dazed until his friends lifted him off my cock.

Rudy fucked Samuel and after he shot his load into Sam's ass got Tommy to screw him too. Once Tommy came, Samuel remounted my cock. He was really open by then and he got seven inches. I have no desire to hurt anyone, so I let the dwarf set his own pace. Samuel was bouncing on my cock when he shot off, Roman candle style. We all took a break.

They were an affable group and excited about the play. Casting dwarfs as fairies was common, but using dwarfs as Oberon and Titania were unusual. Often children played these roles. For a dwarf to play the role was a major opportunity for the little men. Since I was new to the cast, I asked if there were any members I should watch out for.

"It's a good group in general," Rudy said. "For some reason some are tense and on edge. At first, I thought it was acting with little people, but I don't think that's the problem. One of the mechanicals is a bit odd."

"What do you mean?"

"It's Robert, who's playing Flute," David said. "He whines about not playing Lysander, the romantic lead. He'd be unattractive even if he didn't have acne. Not much of an actor either."

"The two female leads have a problem. Bruce and Mark are a pair of flaming queens who don't like the idea of sharing a kingdom," Samuel said. "They think the stage isn't big enough for two queens."

"Little do they know a third queen may carry the day," Tommy said looking directly at Samuel.

"I may be a queen, but I do my part," Samuel said. "I play my role straight."

"How straight can that be?" David asked.

"Some of us are men playing women because it was a convention of the stage at that period," Samuel said. "Sometimes men play women for comic effect. It's important that I not be comic until I have the big scene with Bottom."

"Is Lance in the Queen competition?" I asked.

"He's a nice boy," Samuel said. "He's just having fun, not trying to undermine another actor."

"Acting troops seem to be awash in intrigue and rivalries," I observed.

"Actually this is better than most," Rudy said. "Charlie is a thoughtful director and respectful. I can tell you he's been very good about we little people. Sometimes we are treated on the level of the trained dogs or animal acts. He's demanding, but good. I think he's on his way up. Queen Macbeth was a success. If this play works, he may move up."

We had a few beers as we talked. My cock was at their mouth's level most of the time and they all liked to take a passing lick. The men recharged after the earlier orgasms. This time we had a hot foursome done mostly for my benefit. They wanted to get me off. Rudy, who I knew from before, took my entire cock up his ass. He was a good sport and we really got into it. I was on my back when he sat on it, but a doggy style interlude really rocked his boat.

In that position, David fucked me again and I got to suck Samuel and Tommy's meat as I slowly pumped my cock into Rudy's innards. I liked Tommy's precum. I loved his cream. I shot off as I fucked Rudy and David deposited his load in my hole. I sat up when David came, with Rudy still impaled on my cock. Samuel sucked Rudy and took his load.

Rudy had a spectacular orgasm, his whole body twitched and shivered as he ejaculated. My cock liked that and I pumped a second load into Rudy's quivering ass. Overall, it was a great success.

# Part 2

The next morning, I went to see a neighbor who had recently retired as Dean of Faculty at William Byrd University. At least half of the actors were graduates of William Byrd. Dean Doveton knew just about all there was to know about the school.

I told him about the poison pen letters. He knew all about it. Actually, he knew nothing about it, but there had been a previous outbreak in the Drama Department in the Performing Arts School.

"No one mentioned that," I said.

"It was eight years ago. There have been two generations of students since then," Dean Doveton said. "We worked hard to keep it out of the news. It was embarrassing and the people who got the letters kept it quiet. There were slashed tires and a smoke bomb or two. It was nasty business."

"Can you give me details?"

Dean Doveton was quiet as he thought it over. "I'll tell you all I know if you use only what is necessary. It could still be embarrassing," he said. "The letters accused faculty members of having homosexual relations with their students, orgies as well. The students got letters accusing them of seducing their teachers. The letters said they would give this information to the newspapers and to the General Assembly. The letters to the students said they would tell their parents."

"The parents didn't know the sexual preferences of their kids?"

"The parents never know," Dean Doveton said. "By the way, a good portion of the recipients weren't gay. One male faculty member had been disciplined for getting too close to a female student. The man was a flaming heterosexual. The letters were nasty and shocking, very ugly. There was one attempted suicide attempt. A young student took an overdose. She was terrified her parents would disown her."

"Did you find out who sent the letters?"

"Not exactly. Several of the principal players left Richmond and the letters stopped," he said. "It could have been either of them or one of their devotees. We were so relieved they stopped, we didn't do any more investigation."

"Did you find out what generated the problem?"

"Do you know Professor Kirkland from Art History?" the Dean asked, "He was the faculty member who investigated the problem. He wrote a confidential report. He can give you all the details." I had met him several years earlier. It had been in a social situation. The Dean called him and clued him in. He was free after three that afternoon. I was to meet him at Professor Kirkland's apartment.

Rehearsals started at 7:00 so I had time.

Kirkland was a 60-year-old giant, at least six feet four. We had met years earlier in a mutual friend's hot tub. He was as well-endowed as me. I might have been a little longer and he was a little thicker. Mine looks bigger because of my undersized body. Kirkland and I traded size queen stories. He lived in a well-renovated carriage house off Monument Avenue.

When I got there, he greeted me warmly and then introduced me to his partner Stanford. Stanford was maybe ten years younger than Kirkland. He was an executive dressed in a suit and tie. Kirkland was every inch a professor and he gave me a well-prepared lecture on the poison pen event.

"The former chairman, Gustav Schmidt was fired after a policy dispute with the Dean. Schmidt was tenured, so he remained on the faculty even though he was no longer the chair. He came to believe he was the victim of a homosexual plot to remove him from power and to replace him with a gay man."

"How does a guy who doesn't like gays get to be a chairman of a drama department?" I asked.

"That's not at all clear," Kirkland said, "He never had any problems with gay faculty before. Schmidt wasn't able to admit his own actions had anything to do with losing his position. I think he searched for a scapegoat and found the gay members of his faculty available. He had supporters too. They were jokingly referred to as Gustav's Groupies."

"In Gustav's defense, several of the female groupies were troubled. All were unmarried and had no boyfriends. Like Gustav they couldn't believe they personally had any responsibility for their lack of success at love."

"Ugly as sin?" I asked.

"No. I interviewed most of them always with my secretary in attendance. She thought the main problem was shitty attitude. They had a chip on their shoulders the size of Texas," Kirkland said. "Gustav had one major failing. He was an amateur mental health counselor. When a student had a problem, he wanted to help them himself. Some needed professional help. That might have been related to the letters."

Kirkland gave me the low down on the incident. The combination of mental illness and revenge could easily result in poison pen letters.

"Do you remember the Globe Theater Project of three, or four years ago?" Stanford asked. He had been sitting and listening.

"I vaguely recall the name," I said.

"It made a big splash, but its first production, Hamlet, crashed and burned," Stanford asked. "There was a very public airing of dirty linen after that. As I recall, someone mugged the man playing Hamlet. I think the stage manager was the victim of a hit and run driver too. It struck me as odd that two members of the company were crime victims. Statistically improbable."

"Are you an accountant by any chance?" I asked.

"I work for the state in statistical analysis," Stanford explained. "I work in crime statistics."

"I'll check on that," I said. We talked for a while and I got ready to leave.

"Clydesdale I remember our last meeting," Kirkland said, "You made an impression on me. I told Stanford about you and he was impressed. Stanford has an interest in…"

"Size?" I filled in the missing word.

"Are you offended?" he asked.

"Not at all," I said. "Would you be offended if I said I have an interest in willing bottoms?"

"It looks to me like this might be everyone's lucky day," Stanford said. "Let's adjourn to the bedroom."

"Is this all right with you?" I asked of Kirkland.

He smiled. "I have an interest in size too," he said. "I promised Stanford if I ever found a cock as big as mine I'd bring it home. Oh, by the way, I said I'd bring the guy who possessed the cock home too!"

"That's a relief," I said. We stripped. Kirkland put on a porn DVD. Stanford was of average height and weight, bald and hairy. He was also very interested. Kirkland was bald and hairy too. He put his arm around my shoulders and stroked the hair on my back. Stanford got on his knees and sucked us both. We were both uncut and soft. I hadn't run into a skin fancier in a while. Stanford liked foreskin and was into it big time.

Skin fanciers only have a short window of opportunity. The better they suck the shorter the time they have to play. Stanford was evenhanded and our knobs pushed free of the skin at about the same time. I had thought Kirkland's was thicker and mine was longer, but up close and fully aroused, it wasn't clear. He had a big mushroom head, flared and purple-pink. It was almost iridescent. His slit was wide and already moist.

I must admit Stanford was genuinely enthusiastic about my cock.

"I'd love to suck your cock," I said to Kirkland. We rearranged ourselves. Kirkland sat on the edge of the bed. I sucked him as Stanford scooted under me to do his part. We all got excited.

"Are you sure you want to see my cock in Stanford's ass?" I asked.

"I'm kind of turned on by it," he said. "I'm a bit of a size queen myself. Would you mind if I opened Stanford up first?"

"Be my guest, anything that makes it easier is fine with me," I said. "I'll lubricate him for you, if you want?" Kirkland smiled. Stanford sucked on Kirkland's cock as I opened his ass.

"How often do you get fucked?" I asked.

"Four or five times a week," Stanford said. "Unless I get lucky, that is."

"You're real tight for an ass which is so experienced," I said. "Do you ever trade places?"

"I like to bottom, but not as much as Stanford likes it," Kirkland said. "He used to fuck me, but the more I fuck him the more he wants to be fucked." I had two fingers in Stanford's ass. It was clear his prostate was a major sex organ for him. With one hand in Stanford's hole, I used my other hand to coat his lover's cock with lube.

Stanford laid back and hoisted his legs. Kirkland grabbed the legs and spread them wide. The hole was wide open and defenseless. A second later Kirkland's cock head nuzzled in the juicy ass. A bottle of poppers sat on the side table. I got them ready.

The older man bounced a few times and slowly pushed his huge knob into the tight hole. I got the bottle. Kirkland smiled. I opened the poppers and gave Stanford a snort. He shivered and his partner's purple knob vanished into his love tunnel. A few minutes later, he was fully impaled in the huge cock, and was loving it.

After the slow entry, the pace picked up. Kirkland evolved from a slow and easy lover to a man rammer. Stanford's eyes rolled back into his head and he zoned out.

"Damn, I was getting carried away," Kirkland said as he pulled away. He left his head in the ass. You could tell both men loved the sexual connection. I could also tell Kirkland was having a hard time pulling out. Several times, he pulled away, but he never pulled the head out.

"Cum is a great lubricant," I said.

"You don't mind sloppy seconds?" Kirkland asked.

"Not it all," I said. "Do you mind if I shoot my load in Stanford's ass too?"

"Please!" Stanford moaned. Kirkland smiled and fucked hard. I gave both men the bottle of poppers. It was only a few strokes later when they popped. I lubricated my cock as Kirkland ejaculated. Stanford's ass was dilated when Kirkland finally pulled out. I could see into the love tunnel and the glistening man seed. I was ready to move in.

Remarkably, by the time my knob was at his ass, it had closed up. I knew his sphincter had been stretched wide by Kirkland not once, but maybe hundreds of times. Still, his ass was tight and resisted my entry. I had the poppers in my hand and gave it to Stanford. My head was in on the next thrust and half my shaft slid in on the next.

It was as if an electric jolt struck Stanford. I was still and let him adjust to my cock. He began to rotate his hips. I pushed the rest of my cock up his chute. The sperm filled tunnel shivered as I went deep. Stanford was moaning and gasping for air. When he caught his breath, he was a welcoming and active bottom. I enjoyed it, but there was no way I could have enjoyed it as much as Stanford was.

After about ten minutes, Kirkland tapped me on the shoulder and went in for a second time. He and I traded places a few times over the next hour. We did Stanford doggy style a few times too. The last time I fucked him, I was thinking poor Stanford was looking a bit frayed. My cock took mercy on him and I had a top of the line orgasm. It was both long and pleasurable. The warm cream inside his raw ass did the trick for Stanford. He shot off too.

Kirkland would need to change the sheets and wash off the wall, after that one. It was lovely. I pulled out and licked up some of Stanford sperm to help a little. I had to get to the rehearsal so I got dressed.

"Do you ever bottom?" Kirkland asked me as we went to the door.

"Sometimes."

"I do too. I've never been fucked by anyone as big as you," Kirkland said.

"You're curious?" I asked. He nodded.

"Maybe we could do this again," he observed. "It was better than I had guessed for Stanford and for me."

"I'd like that," I said. "I'm curious too."

The rehearsal was a bit anti climatic after the visit to Kirkland and Stanford, but it was productive.

We mechanicals did a run through of our first scene. Santa was spectacular. Fred was made for the over the top role like Bottom.

One of my fellow Rustics was a handsome young man named Danny. He played Snug, the joiner. Snug played the lion and had even fewer lines than me. Danny had a knack for turning his face into a vacant expression, turning from a lively boy into a dolt. He also had a knack for slapstick. I wondered why he hadn't been selected for one of the romantic roles. He was bearded and had a hairy chest.

Robert, the actor was playing Flute, played Thisbe, the hero of the play within the play. He complained the role was beneath him, but read his lines. He had lots of lines compared to the rest of us rustics, other than Fred.  He was the only one of the rustics to be unenthusiastic. As we rehearsed the two queens, Bruce and Mark, who were playing Hermia and Helena, seemed to be on the edge of outright war.  Charlie kept on giving them disapproving glances.  They got the message.

The dwarfs had warned me about Bruce and Mark.  Both men were handsome in a 1930s lounge lizard way.  By my way of thinking, they weren't handsome enough to be that unpleasant.

Fred moved on from his rehearsal with us, to his transformation into an ass accomplished by a magic potion.  Frankly, I'm not much into magic potions and this part of the play seemed foolish.  Fred was spectacular and turned the scene into a rolling on the floor it was so funny event. He subtly introduced donkey mannerisms and characteristics that accomplished the transformation without costumes.

The big love scene between Bottom, now transformed into an ass, and Titania, queen of a fairies, played by Samuel the dwarf was wonderful. Titania was a victim of another potion that made her fall in love with the first person she saw.  Samuel was perfect in the role of the love struck Queen.  I didn't know how close the two men were off stage, but it was both comic and oddly believable.

Off to the side a man I didn't know was taking with Charlie.  The conversation became animated as the scene came to an end.

"I don't know why anyone would seriously consider regurgitating a meaningless old warhorse like this," the man said.  "We need modern plays that speak to our age!" I couldn't hear Charlie's response.

"It's a weak play any way and you're pandering to cheap emotions. My god, using dwarfs and rednecks!" The man was getting worked up.

"Some people think Shakespeare has held up well," Charlie said.

"The redneck costume looks like shit and you need to find a makeup artist who isn't demeaning to rednecks," he said looking directly at me.

"It ain't no costume, mister," I said. He turned bright red and the cast burst into laughter. The man left the stage.

"Who is that asshole?" I asked.

"He's Milton Hammerly, the theater critic of the newspaper." Charlie said.

"You should have punched him in the nose," David said.

"Shit," I said. "If I punched every asshole I meet in the nose I'd hurt my knuckles." There was more laughter. The rehearsal was over. Danny asked if I like to go out for a beer and a sandwich. That was fine with me. Bruce and Samuel tagged along, as did the quiet guy who played Demetrius, Henry. We went to a small restaurant nearby. I had a beer and ordered a burger.

Apparently, Milton was not a particularly favorite critic. Bruce told me you needed to have a roll in the hay to get a good review out of him. "He likes young men he can help with his career. I'm not that picky, but Milton is scum."

"I'm pleased you draw the line somewhere, Henry said. "I've heard if you ran into a well hung amoeba, you'd give it a try."

"Absolutely untrue!" Bruce protested in a good-humored way. "People spread lies about me. I wouldn't give an amoeba a second look. Unless it was incredibly well hung of course." Without his rival Mark present Bruce was good natured and funny. He complimented Samuel on his acting ability.

"It was hard to believe you weren't in love with Bottom," Bruce said.

"Well, he is a lovable ass," Samuel replied. "How are you going to play Hermia?"

"I was thinking about using Annette Funicello as my model," Bruce replied. As they talked, I saw a big scar on Henry's arm. He noticed I was looking at it.

"Motorcycle accident?" I asked.

"A chance meeting with a car," Henry replied.

"Chance my foot!" Bruce interjected. "It was hit and run and I've never believed it was an accident."

"Were you the guy in Hamlet?" Danny asked.

"I was strictly behind the scenes in that play," Henry said. "I'd rather not talk about it."

"I was strictly a spear carrier in that mess," Bruce said. "Henry deserves the Purple Heart and the Medal of Honor for trying to keep the thing together."

"What are you guys talking about?" Samuel asked.

"It's a long story and I need to get my beauty sleep, lord knows," Bruce said. "But I will tell you everything when I have the time." I took the men to their apartments, since I was the only one with a car. I got the impression several of them were relived to get a ride.

# Part 3

The next morning I looked into the Globe Theater Project and the ill-fated production of Hamlet. One of my neighbors, Bobby Wilmot, loved the theater and he kept clippings, programs and other information on local plays. When I asked him about Hamlet, he got excited.

"It was the play from hell. The director was a new hotshot faculty member at William Byrd and this was his first play. Rumor had it he was going to be the new chairman of the department. Eldon Jones, the Director, was very Avant-guard and modern. I thought he was a bull shitter, but he really impressed some, especially the local drama critics. The build up for the play was massive. There were several articles in the papers and segments on the television stations.

"And how was it?"

"It was a total disaster. The concept sounded good, but was bad on the stage. I just didn't work. Eldon was demanding and treated his actors like shit. He made them bend to his will. He told them their ideas were stupid and immature, but when the play failed he blamed it on them, publicly."

"Publicly?"

"He gave an interview saying the actors were too immature to carry out his brilliant concept," Bobby said. "I've never seen anything like it. You may think that, or even say it to a few close friends, but never in public. Then there was the mugging and the hit and run."

"Are you suspicious about those events?" I asked.

"They are curious," Bobby said. "There is more than that. Ophelia tried to commit suicide. She thought Eldon was in love with her. He savaged her in the newspaper."

"Did that information get out?" I asked.

"No, it was hushed up," Bobby said.

I gave him the list of the players in Midsummer Night Dream. Wilmot checked those who were associated with Hamlet. Bruce and Mark were in the company, but as spear-carriers. Henry was the Stage Manager. Charlie played Polonius. Wilmot provided one unexpected bit of information. Ophelia was now Henry's wife. They had two children.

"Who paid for these two companies?"

"I don't know that, but I can find out pretty easily," he responded. "Whoever backed Hamlet lost big time. It was an expensive production. Of course, almost all plays lose money, but this was a total wipe out. There was considerable ill feeling in the theater community, because it soured potential donors from giving for several years."

"Was the former Drama chairman Gustav Schmidt involved in the Globe Theater Project?"

"Not directly. He hired Eldon of course, but the Globe Project was independent of the University," Wilmot explained."

"Where are Gustav and Eldon now?"

"I don't know, but I can make inquiries," Wilmot said. "I take it you are investigating something?"

"Yes, everything is still preliminary, so there's nothing definite," I said.

"I will ask around. I am a well-known gossip. No one will think anything of it. I'll call if I find something."

I went to my office and had my staff to a quick search on the actors and others involved I took care of some other odd and ends that had accumulated while I was rehearsing. There was no rehearsal that day, but I was to get measured for my costumes.

I met Skyler DeMonville, the costume designer. To say he was gay didn't do him justice. Mega gay or Hyper gay would be closer to the truth. I'm not much into flaming queens, but Skyler was so far beyond that, he sort of took your breath away. He was hyperactive and told me he designed and made the costumes with limited help. He also was fast and got his work done quickly as he chatted at a breakneck speed.

Skyler liked my hairy chest. He had a grand scheme. The lovers and courtiers were to be elegant, sleek and smooth. The rude mechanicals, we rustics, were to be crude and hairy. The fairies were to be dressed in leaves, gossamer fabrics and sequins. "It's a huge cast and the audience can get confused. I want each of the groups in the play to be distinct and clearly defined," Skyler said. "Lord you are a hairy one. That will be good."

"Are all of the rustics hairy?" I asked.

"Not as hairy as you, but hairy enough," he said. "You come with most of your costume growing on your torso. It's convenient and economical."

"I'm glad to accommodate you,"

"I'm not sure what to do with the beard," Skyler mused. "How long will it take for you to grow it longer?"

"A week or two."

Skyler laughed. "You get five o'clock shadow at ten in the morning?" I nodded.

"Maurice! Come here," he yelled. A very small and very effeminate man appeared. "Maurice is the production hair dresser. We're trying to save money on wigs. We'll see what he can do."

"What in hell did the cat drag in?" Maurice asked as he gave me the once over.

"Maurice is a flaming fagot, but he has the sensitivity of a turnip," Skyler explained. "Don't take a word he says seriously. He's a pig."

"I love you too," Maurice said.

"This man presents Wall in our play," Skyler said. "Rough-cast is the phrase the Bard used."

"Rough-cast, that hardly describes him. He needs some ivy to hide the all too obvious defects," Maurice complained.

"Damn it, once and a while you say something intelligent!" Skyler said. "Fetch me some ivy, you worthless churl!" Maurice vanished and returned with a trash bag of plastic ivy.

"Would you take your shirt off," Skyler asked. He wove the ivy into a crown and made a necklace of ivy for my chest. Five minutes later I was ivy covered wall. Skyler was happy. "I think an ivy covered jock will complete it." I looked in the mirror and I was transformed. The effect was clever and comical.

"What about the hole, the cranny?" Maurice asked.

"Maurice has an anal fixation," Skyler declared.

"My fixation isn't enough to let this bit of Rough-cast give me a poke," Maurice said.

"Don't you believe a world of that. Maurice can't pass a fire plug without getting a hard on," Skyler proclaimed. "If it's even vaguely elongated he wants it in his ass."

My fitting was over and I left. I ran into Charlie as I left. "They are quite the pair," I remarked.

"Believe it or not, but they are both are good at what they do."

"Have there been any incidents over night?"

"No letters for several days," Charlie said. "Maybe it's over. Whoever was sending them may have gotten his jollies and has moved on to something new." As we talked the man playing Demetrius, Roland Smith, came over. He hadn't been at the rehearsals due to his Grandmother's funeral.

Roland was tall, dark and handsome. He seemed pleasant and affable. It was hard to believe he and Skyler were the same species. Roland wanted to know what he needed to do to make up for his absence. Everything seemed normal.

The next morning they found Maurice's body at the foot of the balcony stair. He was dead. I didn't hear about it until afternoon.

The police treated it as an accident and not a crime. There was no media coverage.

The crew was shocked. Skyler was devastated. While it was treated as an accident, I didn't believe that for one minute. Kirkland's friend, Stanford, would have described it as statistically improbable. No one in the cast, or crew believed it either. While they bickered, incessantly Skyler and Maurice were lovers. Apparently, it was a mutually agreeable master-slave relationship.

The stage manager told me there was no reason for Maurice to go up the stairs he was supposed to have fallen down. "Maurice stayed in the costume shop and almost never left it. It's hard to believe he had any reason to go to the balcony." I called Bobby Wilmot to see what he knew about Skyler and Maurice.

"Skyler's a character, but genuinely talented and driven. His costumes are always done on time. He was involved in the Hamlet disaster. He was fired because he wouldn't do what the director wanted."

"Isn't that his job? To do what the director wanted?" I asked.

"To a point, the costumes weren't workable," Bobby explained. "It was physically difficult for the actors to move inside them. The reviewers mentioned the wooden acting in the play. Much of that was due to the costumes."

Rather to my surprise, Skyler was a "the show must go on" man. He took a day off for the funeral, but that was it. Several days later, he had my costume finished and I went in for a fitting. It wasn't so much as a fitting as an attaching. He had the pieces ready, but wasn't sure how to attach them to my body.

I stripped off my shirt and got down to my shorts. "I hope you aren't a really modest guy, but you are going to need to take more off," Skyler said. "You need to wear my souped-up jock." I took off my shorts. The jock was one-step more modest than being naked. It was covered in ivy, but lined in silk, next came grassy boots. They had vines that went up my legs and attached to the jock.

One of the vines was actually a suspender that went over my shoulder and down my back. It kept the jock from sagging under the weight of the ivy. Skyler now greatly embellished the crown from my first fitting was and it had birds in it. There were buttons in the jock to make the birds sing. The whole contraption was pretty cool. He told me to walk. Several things poked me, so he adjusted them.

Throughout the entire fitting, Skyler never copped a feel, or fondled my equipment. I was shocked. I went to a rehearsal of the Pyramus and Thisbe play after the fitting. This was more of a costume run through. Dress rehearsal was weeks away, but Charlie and Skyler wanted to make sure the unusual costumes worked. It was spectacular. The collection of hairy rustics struck just the right tone for the farce. We had to stop a few times the crew was laughing so hard.

Fred is a hairy Polar Bear. He was wearing a kilt, a big horsehair Classical Greek helmet and armor. The armor was made of tortoise shells unconvincingly tied together. Robert, who played Thisbe, was in a grass skirt with squash gourd breasts. The costumes were imaginative, funny and oddly attractive.

Afterward in the dressing room, it took a while to undress me and then no one there missed an opportunity to cop a feel or make a comment. It sounds stupid, but I was relieved my cock hadn't lost its magic. Even Robert was interested. I've always said there's a world of difference between a redneck and a big dicked redneck.

As I left Skyler came up to me. "Would you like to get together and have a glass of wine?"

"I need to get something to eat," I said.

"Well I can solve that problem," Skyler said. "Follow me; my apartment is just around the corner. I will whip up something fast and good."

His apartment was very nice. It looked like something you'd find in a fancy magazine. He also made a good dinner. He broiled two steaks and made a salad. Skyler was all business while he cooked, but we talked about the play during dinner. The conversation turned to the poison pen letters afterward.

"I assume you are investigating the letters," he said. "You aren't fooled by Maurice's death are you?"

"It doesn't smell good," I said. "Murder seems extreme."

"You're right about that. I thought the writer was a bitter hyper-sensitive artistic type who turned nasty," Skyler said. "Nasty is one thing; murder is another."

"Did Maurice have enemies?"

"Maurice was harmless. He had spats. No one paid any attention to him, except for me, of course," he said.

"You had spats too?"

"That was a game. Maurice had what we would now call an esteem problem. He insulted people before they had a chance to insult him," Skyler said. "Verbal abuse turned him on. It was a quirk. We would fight all day and I'd fuck him silly all night. It was a satisfactory arrangement for both of us. He was a size queen. I was the biggest man he had met. He thought he had died and gone to heaven when I fucked him the first time."

"He was a good bottom?"

"You must know what it's like when you find someone who can take your cock and enjoy it. He just loved it," Skyler said. "If he knew you were hung, he'd have loved you. I discovered you a few days too late."

"I wasn't his type."

"I hate to sound tacky, but your cock is his type."

I laughed. "I've run into that a few times before. I don't mind curiosity. You were good doing the fitting. You don't mix business and pleasure?"

"Genitals and costume design are a bad combination," Skyler said. "It's unethical. Actors can get really jumpy if they think you're going to jump them."

I smiled. "You're right about that."

"Through the grapevine I've heard you aren't opposed to a little show and tell," Skyler said.

"You heard wrong. I never tell."

"If I changed it to a show and taste would it be of more interest to you?" Skyler asked. I began to unbutton my shirt.

It was hard to believe how fast Skyler stripped. One minute he was dressed, the next minute he was nude. I had no idea what he would look like naked. He was tall, slim and quite muscular. He looked like a swimmer, or a dancer. He was shaved, except for his bush and genitals. They were natural. He had blond hair on his head, but his pubes were black. His skin was pale, but healthy looking. His large pink tits and cock head provided the only color. The head was pinkish purple. The cock itself was seven or eight inches long in a relaxed state.

He was attractive and masculine. He was as masculine as a guy as elegant as he could be. The only discordant aspect of his body was his balls. Skyler had Godzilla's balls. They were huge and contained in a hairy, low hanging sack. I guessed his cock was longer than mine was, but I was thicker. I wouldn't know until he got hard.

I cupped them in my hand. "Pretty," I said. "You have the meat and potatoes."

Skyler smiled. "I like smooth men," he said, "but I could never get a razor near my family jewels. Maurice wanted me to shave my bush, but I wouldn't do it."

"He was smaller than I am. Did he have any problem taking it?" I asked as I stroked his cock. A bead of precum emerged from the slit. Touched it with my finger and spread it over his knob.

"He said it was hard to take, but he always came back," Skyler said. He had peeled my foreskin back to expose my head. "Can I lick it?" he asked.

"Sure," I said. "I leak a lot. Do you like cock juices?"

"Maurice drooled like a leaky faucet," he said as took my cock into his mouth. Skyler wept as he licked and sucked my cock. My cock drool seemed to being back memories of his late lover. No one had talked to him about Maurice beyond the normal conventional condolences. Sex was at the core of their friendship and no one talked about that and how much he had lost.

I asked him if Maurice had a tight hole, and did it open and relax as the night wore on. Then I asked if he shot his load in the ass or down his throat. Skyler wanted to talk.

"He loved it in the ass," Skyler reminisced, "He was totally passive. If I had a friend over we'd both fuck him. He'd beg until he got you up his ass. We went to a party once where everyone took their turn.

When we got home, I fucked him again. It was like churning butter. Have you ever used your pals' cum as lubricant?"

"A few times," I said. "Sperm is good lube. It may sound funny, but it was a turn on when I knew my pals made it in their balls. Call me a romantic."

Skyler laughed. "I felt the same way. It's messy, but exciting. By the way, your cock drool is tasty."

"Thanks. Good sex can be messy. That doesn't bother me much. I don't need to look my best to have a good time," I said. We got on his bed so we could sixty-nine. He must have been 12 inches. His cock was meaty, but I was able to deep throat him. I must have suctioned a pint of precum from his balls as I pulled back.

"I hate mess. I'm too much of a control freak," he said. "Could you do that again? It was great."

I felt a bit like a suckling pig on a spit, but I did it again. He tried to do the same, but I was too thick. He did do his best and I appreciated the effort. I deep throated him again and this time I smelled the aroma of lubricant coming from his hole.

I got my finger at his ass hole and played with his slippery sphincter. "Were you expecting company?" I asked.

"I don't know what I was expecting," Skyler said. He may not have been expecting, but he had a hope. Skyler didn't know he was a bottom for another fifteen minutes. It took that long to get in. He had lots of lube and poppers to ease the way. Once I was in, I took the poppers and I fucked him silly.

# Part 4

I'm not sure I've ever fucked a man as grief therapy, but that comes close to being what I did for Skyler. In some ways, he was taking my cock for Maurice. Skyler was normally a top, but he wanted to feel what Maurice felt. The costume designer was ill at ease when I first entered his ass. After five minutes, he relaxed and after ten, he surrendered and let my cock work its magic. He was doing a good imitation of a bottom pig by the time I shot off.

"Breed me!" he whined and whimpered. Breed him I did. I almost expected to see some of my cock juices spurting from his ears I shot so much. He climaxed too, so we were stuck together with his cum as glue. I collapsed on him in post orgasm exhaustion. My cock was still in his ass and Skyler was nice enough to squeeze his sphincter to get the last drops from my balls. This was enough to inspire a few more ejaculations.

I showered and went home. The next day I got flowers delivered to my apartment with a note that said thank you. I knew where they came from. That morning I also got a visit from a Detective Dean Willard of the Richmond police. He was new to the force; I hadn't met him before.

"Are you the guy they call the Redneck Sherlock Holmes?" he asked.

"Well, they certainly have the Redneck part right."

He laughed. "One of my men said you were hanging around the Midsummer Night's Dream set. Can I ask you why? He didn't think it was because you felt a need to express your artistic nature."

"I'll tell you all, but I prefer to trade information. Do you have anything worrying you about Maurice's death?"

"He had bruises on his neck and wrists," Willard said, "Not at all consistent with a fall."

I told him the whole story. It was clear after I finished recounting the story Willard was going to be helpful. He had withheld the autopsy report to give him time to investigate. He didn't want news of the murder to leak out prematurely.

"The Richmond Police have no ability to go undercover in a theater troop," Dean said. "We're good on drug dealers, but no one can mix with artistic types. I don't know how you got in that group?"

"I'm a flexible guy," I said. "It helps that I'm hung like a horse and open minded. Let me guess, you were a linebacker in college, then the Marine Corps, and a degree in law enforcement?"

"I was a Navy Seal," Dean said. He was built and in good shape, Dean had a flattop that concealed a bald spot and a bristly mustache. With blue eyes and a good tan, the bull like man was impressive. He was born to be a policeman. When I mentioned hung like a horse to take a quick glance at my basket. I was wearing old jeans and the wear marks told all.

"You don't think I'd make a good undercover officer?" he asked. Dean smiled. "I take it the less under covered you are the more popular you become?"

I laughed. "If you saw my costume for the play you would know all!" After that interlude, we got down to business. He would increase foot patrols in the area of the theater and would check up in police records the backgrounds of the people involved. I would keep him aware of any new developments.

I spent the rest of the day in rehearsals. Charlie was a stickler for pronunciation and natural speech. He and the voice person worked with the actors on being intelligible. I had been using my High School Shakespeare as a singsong like recitation. We had done Julius Caesar and Macbeth. The stories were good, but the plays itself were partially unintelligible to me. This was very different. The three groups, the courtiers, the fairies and the rustics would each have a 45 minutes session with the voice coach and then practice while the next group met with the voice coach.

I know rehearsals are supposed to be boring, but I thought they were interesting. It helped that Freddy was there. He knew Shakespeare forwards and backwards and was a one man Cliff notes. He was particularly good about the off color, or borderline obscene references. "They were to appeal to the common man," he explained.

"Well they appeal to me too," I said.

"As far as I can tell they appealed to everyone," Freddy said. "I'm pretty sure Queen Elizabeth laughed as hard as anyone else. I suspect the "appeal to the common man" was a Victorian interpretation intended to appeal to that age's fear of sex. Dr. Bowdler revised the plays to hide the "dirty" parts. He also took the sex out of the Bible, but I've never been sure anyone used the Bible as a sex manual."

The courtiers were having the most problems, so we had the next day off so Charlie could spend the entire day working with them. I got a call from Bobby Wilmot. He had located Eldon Jones, the director of the ill-fated Hamlet and Gustav Schmidt. Wilmot was going to have them over for drinks after a special benefit matinee performance of Guys & Dolls. The benefit was sponsored by the First Lady of Virginia's favorite charity so the Governor and First lady were there. I was invited to post performance party at Wilmot's house.

The party was posh event. There was a series of post-show cocktail parties where the charity would ask for additional contributions. I was looking shaggy since I was growing out my beard for the play, but I put my good suit on and was presentable. I was introduced to the guests as the man-presenting wall in the Midsummer's Night's Dream. That caused considerable merriment.

I met Gustav Schmidt at the door. He was wearing a silk jacket and an ascot. I got the impression he was doing an imitation of a 1930's era director. He had a slight English accent, but it was obviously a stage accent, otherwise he was normal. He didn't strike me as a leader of men.

He asked me about the play. We talked for a while and he seemed to be genuinely interested and friendly. He told me he missed acting and the theater. He had a bad spell a few years earlier and had burned his bridges.

"What happened?" I asked.

"I don't know if you can suffer from temporary paranoia, but I had it. Several things happened all at once and I came to some bad conclusions," he said.

"How are things now?" I asked.

"Good. I'm working in a job I like and things have straightened out." he said.

"It's hard to rebuild the bridges?"

Gustav nodded. Wilmot came over to me with a friend he wanted me to meet. A little later, I met Eldon Jones. He was teaching theater in a local Community College. Short and stocky, he looked more like a longshoreman than a director. He was from Jersey and you could tell. He had several followers with him. He seemed to move with an entourage. The girls had an adoring look I found unsettling. One of the boys with him had the same look.

Twenty-year-olds can be so self-absorbed they don't notice the obvious. Tony must have liked the worship. He didn't mind any damage it might cause when they discovered he had no interest in them. I know a user when I see one.

After a while, I realized he was playing a role. He was trying for Marlon Brando. He liked to play the macho type. He was freely dropping names and insults. It was also clear he was not a forgive and forget man. He was an energetic and engaging man, if you didn't notice the undertones. Eldon was particularly nasty about the newspaper's theater critic, Milton Hammerly. Milton was talking to some people well within hearing distance.

The two men seemed to generate an aura of ill feeling. The rest of the party was cheerful and pleasant, but a cloud hung over them. Wilmot was the perfect host and he separated the warring parties. "Eldon, you need to meet Sally White. She's new to town and wants to meet the local luminaries," he said as he steered Eldon to the other side of the room.

"No one really knows him. They can't appreciate him. He's too talented for Richmond," one of Eldon's young women said.

"I've got that problem too," I said with a smile.

"You're in the theater?" she asked, obviously skeptical.

"I'm playing the wall in Midsummer's Night's Dream," I said. The girl looked puzzled.

"Shakespeare?"

"Oh, I don't do old fashioned plays," she said. "Most of my work has been in experimental-theater."

"I was born to play the wall," I said.

"Eldon's a real man," she said, returning to her original theme. "There are so many fags in the theater. Eldon says it takes a man to play a man."

"What does it take to play a wall?"

"I don't know, but you're too ugly to be a fag," she said. "Has anyone ever told you that you sound like Sam Elliot?"

"Not recently. Is he from Southside Virginia?" I asked. The girl didn't have a sense of humor. She went off to see a friend. I assume she was going talk about experimental theater. The girl was pretentious, clueless and unaware. She was the perfect person to be taken in by a man like Eldon.

I talked with one of Eldon's boys next. Rufus was 23 and much like the girl. He wanted a hero and a mentor. He also thought he was straight. After a few minutes of conversation, I suspected otherwise. He was polite and had heard of the Shakespeare production. He was interested in the play. I explained the handsome courtiers, dwarf fairies and hairy, rude mechanicals scheme. That made sense to him. I described the costumes.

"You're hairy?" Rufus asked. I nodded. "I'm kind of hairy too. My friends say it's gross."

"You need better friends," I said. "We all get the cards we're dealt."

"Well, I'm really hairy," Rufus said as he leaned close to me. We talked for a while and drank quite a bit. I was sitting on a chair when a waiter tripped and covered me with shrimp and cocktail sauce. The sauce that missed me splattered on Rufus. The waiter was apologetic, but I had to get the stuff out of my hair. I had a feeling horseradish would be hard on my eyes if it dripped into them. I had to get home and shower.

"Come by for a night cap," I said. "I only live a block away. You can clean up there if you want." Rufus was willing. We went in the side door of my apartment. I live above my offices. Rufus didn't know I was a detective.

Rufus liked my apartment. As soon as we got in, I offered him a beer. Then we went to the shower to strip and shower. He joined me. My shower is all ornamental ceramic tile featuring tropical plants and parrots in brilliant colors. It looks like a Hollywood star's dream bath. Rufus loved it. It told him about the tile man who owned the building and was stuck with the tile when a client didn't want it.

Rufus seemed like a nice kid, but he had what they call body issues on the TV programs. He was tall, thin and hairy. He thought he looked like a scrawny, hairy scarecrow. I pointed out that half the men in the country would love to be as slim as he was. He thought he was hairy, but when he saw me, he realized there were much hairier men in the world. I told him I associated being hairy with being masculine.

"The hair isn't the only masculine thing about you," Rufus said as he looked at my cock.

I smiled. "You're nicely equipped yourself," I said. "You're a couple notches above standard issue."

"What is standard issue?" he asked. "I've never known."

"I think six inches hard is the usual rule of thumb. Soft it can be just about anything."

"What are you?" he asked.

"Somewhere between 9.5" and 10.5" depending on inspiration," I said. "Guys tell me it's the diameter that is impressive."

"Guys?" Rufus asked.

"100% men," I said, "They seem to appreciate it."

"Oh," he said. His cock began to firm up. He wanted to be matter of fact about my sexual inclinations, but his cock had another idea. He looked down and saw he was getting hard.

"Sorry about that," he said. "I didn't mean to get hard." He was silent for a little while. "Yours is big now. It must be huge when it's hard?"

"I hate to get it cocked and ready with nowhere to shoot it," I said. "You've been drinking. I don't mind getting it up and having some fun, but I don't like solo performances. Are you into it? Are you into cock play?"

"I don't know," he said. Rufus looked at his cock again. He was fully erect. "My cock has a decided preference. I think I drank a little too much to get my nerve up. I noticed your basket at the party."

I smiled. Rufus finally let his cock do his thinking for him. He came over to me and cupped my balls in his hand. I stroked his cock and then dropped to my knees and sucked him. His cock twitched and I got a glob of cum in my mouth.

"Calm down," I said, "Hold back." Remarkably, he held back. The next time I licked his knob pre cum oozed from it. All was well. Being in the shower was good for someone who's trying out man sex for the first time. It was clean and sanitary. When I got up to take a breath, he went down to sample my cock. That was a successful experiment. We dried off and went to my bed.

Rufus was a quick learner and soon became enthusiastic. I'm afraid his straight days ended the first time his mouth came in contact with my cock. Some men think of my cock as a curiosity. They like to look at it and perhaps use it, but that is all. Others are all but transfixed by it. They love it. Rufus was clearly in the later camp.

He made the virgin to cock hound transition in record time. Fortunately, I found out it was purely a sexual attraction. He loved it, not me. I wasn't his type. Wild sex is easy to deal with; puppy love is much harder. Rufus was dealing with a sexual storm of emotion. That was good for him and for me.

Eventually I sat on his cock. I didn't want to fuck him the first night. That would be too much. He was a solid and thick seven and it was good for me, but great for him. He played with my cock while I did a little dance on his meat.

Once his cock was deep in my ass, Rufus wanted to talk. He was attracted to Eldon but had noticed some unattractive things about him. Eldon attracted followers, but he didn't seem to remain on good terms with them for long. Eldon had been teaching at a large high school and there had been some sort of a problem with a girl. "Eldon said the girl had fantasies, but it was nasty," Rufus said. "She thought she was star material, but he sent a bad recommendation for a college. It kept her from getting into the school she wanted."

"Those things are confidential, aren't they?"

"Yes, but one of his former student betrayed him," Rufus said. "He says a man as talented as he is makes enemies. He says he'll get the guy who screwed him."

"I think I know some talented men who have lots of friends," I remarked. Rufus was not too happy about that comment, so I wiggled my hips and he forgot as my warm ass caressed his bloated cock.

"I don't believe this is happening to me," he moaned.

"Do you want me to stop?"

"Shit no!" he cried. I had guessed that.

"Is this your first time?" I asked.

"Yes. I don't think I knew you could do this stuff. I thought sex would be good, but not this good."

"It is bad policy to let the little brain in your cock do your thinking for you all the time, but once in a while you have to let go. That little brain in your cock head has it place. Some men can't relax enough to enjoy sex. You're lucky. You can relax and let your cock be your guide. It opens up a world of pleasure."

"I can't hold off much longer," Rufus said.

"You don't need to. Just relax and let nature take its course. I'm close too."

We made it another five minutes. I was afraid Rufus would get dehydrated by the time he finished shooting. I think I had 23 years of repressed boy cum in my ass. It felt good. I got off him and we showered again. I noticed he collected some of the sperm I shot on his chest and licked it up. His cock twitched a little when his tongue touched the quivering semen. He took a second lick.

# Part 5

Rufus turned out to be a nice kid. I converted him from a virgin to a slut, but more importantly, he learned being an asshole wasn't a good attitude to be emulated. He discovered the asshole was a sex organ to be used. As he left, he had an odd look. I saw it as the hero-worshiping look he had when Eldon was in the room. I told him I wasn't much into love.

"You like sex though?" he asked with a worried look on his face.

"I sure do," I said. "I never get tired of it and I'd like to have few more play sessions with you." Rufus laughed and left with a smile. He was sensible enough to take sex without strings. Rufus was the kind of boy who had great enthusiasms, but he wasn't a fool. He had noticed Eldon had a dark side. He was able to ignore them for a while, but he knew it was there and he wasn't a blind follower. He certainly wasn't going to drink the Kool-Aid when the leader told him too. The girl I had met with Tony wasn't so lucky. I found out her name was Emma.

Later, I asked Skyler if he knew anything about Emma and Eldon. He knew all about her. "She played Rosencrantz in Hamlet. They didn't have enough men to fill all the male roles," he said. "It's not a major role, but she screwed it up. She has a serious problem with over acting. If she were playing your role as the wall, she'd try to do it like Gloria Swanson in Sunset Boulevard. I don't know if Eldon ever screwed her, but she's more than willing."

"Would she be capable of sending the poison pen letters?" I asked.

Skyler looked shocked. After a pause he spoke. "That is a possibility. She was really attached to Eldon in an unhealthy way. She is the kind of person who fades into the scenery. You never notice she's there, but she's always around."

"Was she at Byrd when they had the problems at the Drama Department?" I asked.

"I'm not positive, but it's possible," Skyler said. "As a matter of fact, I think I saw her in a college production of Antony and Cleopatra, she was Charmian, the maid. I think she was replaced when she screwed up. She seemed to think the play was Antony and Charmian. She also had a nasty fight with Ophelia in the production of Hamlet. Emma accused her of making passes at Eldon to get the role."

"What does she do now?"

"I have no idea," Skyler said.

That question was answered for me at lunch. I went to a local burger joint with Freddy and the elves. Emma was waiting tables. She didn't seem to recognize me. She didn't serve us quickly. A waiter showed up fifteen minutes later and apologized. "One of the waitresses got sick and had to leave. Sorry to make you wait," he said. We ordered and got fast service. He got a good tip from Freddy.

Neither Fred nor any of the dwarfs had gotten a letter, so it was clearly a local problem. Samuel was a classic gossip and got along well with most of the crew. I told him I wanted to know more about Eldon and Emma. It was the fairies night to rehearse so they went to the theater.

As I was about to get up, Detective Willard came in with an old friend of mine, Frank. Frank had worked with me for several years before he became a detective who did mostly white-collar crime. He was an accountant and was good with financial scams. I asked them to join me. I had a cup of coffee while they ate.

Dean slipped me a note saying he wanted to meet with me later. After dinner, we went to my apartment. "As I assume you guessed, someone murdered Maurice," Dean said. "There was no question after the Medical Examiner's report. He was strangled, but thrown down the stairs while he was still alive. The Examiner thought he might well have been unconscious."

"Attacked from behind?"

"That is her guess. Maurice wasn't a strong man anyway. There were no injuries suggesting he tried to slow the fall or save himself," Dean said. "After our conversation, I got several of the letters from Charlie, the director. "Standard ink jet printing."

"But, not on standard paper!" Frank said. "The writer fucked up."

"What exactly is non-standard ink jet paper?" I asked.

"Most people get their paper from Staples, or Office Max, but not the Commonwealth of Virginia," Frank said. "They put it out to bid. About eight years ago, the company that got the bid substituted another paper for the one they provided. It was 70% recycled content and they used a chemical additive to make whiter."

"This is that paper?

"It is. The additive gave people a rash, so it caused a minor scandal. It was recalled," Frank said. "Whoever used it had to have access to the paper between January and August 2001. It was only distributed to colleges and universities. The state itself had enough of the previous paper contract, so they didn't get any before the problem was discovered."

"In Richmond that would be William Byrd and the community college, right?"

Frank nodded. "There was one thing about the font too," he added. "Windows used Ariel or Times New Roman as their standard font. The head of the University's graphics department had a personal problem with Ariel. He liked Helvetica and was pissed at Windows for creating the Ariel rip off. He got the University to adopt his own font as the University standard, something called Virginiana. It was only used on University owned computers."

"So it was done on a University computer?"

"Or a former University computer," Frank said. "All of the 2001 computers have been replaced and the old ones sold as surplus. I went to the sale. Employees and staff had the first choice. It was pretty well picked over by the time I got there."

"When was the sale?"

"2004, the university adopted Windows Vista and the old computers didn't have enough horsepower to run it," Frank said.

Frank had to leave, but as he left he whispered, "If you feel like a little charity work, Dean is ripe for plucking. He had a really bad divorce and now is horny as hell. I have a feeling he's interested in a trip to the wild side."

"What in hell makes you think that?"

"He was asking about you. He heard you have a donkey dong and what to know it that was true. He knew I worked for you," Frank replied, "You don't ask that question unless you have visions of sugarplums dancing in your head. He knows I'm gay, by the way. He's been getting friendly."

"How friendly is friendly?" I asked.

"Not as friendly as you get!" Frank said, smiling. "We've been in the shower at the same time. I think he needs more inspiration than I can give." He winked at me and left. I didn't think I was much in the mood to help the detective get his rocks off. When I returned to the living room, we continued to talk about the case. Dean said he could track down the computer sales. He had a list of everyone associated with the play, or with Hamlet and the previous outbreak of poison pen letters.

Dean connected with the University Police and they had a big file of the earlier letter-writing episode. He also had the complete cast and support staff list of both Hamlet and Midsummer's Night Dream. He could crosscheck them with the records from the computer sale. As we talked, the idea of a roll in the hay seemed to become increasingly attractive.

He went off to the bath to take a leak and came back dazzled. It was that kind of a room and it worked its magic again. The atmosphere changed from being all business to more personal and tense. Dean was inept at turning the conversation into a more personal vein. He was unsure and uneasy. I knew what he wanted, but he had no idea how to get it. Somehow having a needy man in need of relief in front of me brought out my charitable instincts.

He returned the conversation to the bath. "It's so big it's almost another living room," he said.

"I think of it as a play room," I said. "Cleanliness may be next to godliness, but most of the play in my shower isn't godly."

Dean smiled. "Frank said you are a playful guy and you had a lot to play with."

"That I do. Frank didn't tell me if you were playful."

"Does horny count?" Dean asked.

"It helps," I replied. "Let me be direct. I don't mind helping a guy out, but I like to have some fun too. If you are timid, I may not be the man for you. If you want some rip-roaring man sex, that's more my line."

"I'm new at this, but I would like to try more," Dean said.

"Well. Let's adjourn to the shower and see what pops up," I said. Dean had no problem getting naked. He had a good, toned body and nice equipment. He didn't mind showing it off at all. He would cut a good figure in the police locker room. My interests turned from being charitable to plain old lusty. I kind of like filling in the gaps in an uptight military man's sexual education. Dean was curious, but I don't think he knew he was a size queen. I wasn't sure he knew what he was sexually either. I think his bad divorce affected his thinking.

I'm a gay man who loves men and cocks. I had a strong suspicion Dean had a fetish for large cocks. I've known men who liked big breasts, but didn't like women that much. One kid I went to school with didn't really like women at all, but when he saw melon-sized breasts, he went crazy. Fortunately, he married a woman with watermelon breasts. That turned out well.

I'm not sure Dean would have sucked me if I had an average sized cock. As it was, he was almost my slave. He would do anything and wanted just to see it and have contact with it. Actually, it wasn't just the cock he liked. My balls were good too.

We stripped and got under the water. He came over to me and cupped my balls in his hand, then stroked my cock, peeling back the foreskin. He was cut, but was obviously a foreskin fancier. I got hard as a rock. We washed each other. He spent most of his time working on my cock. I made sure his ass was nice and clean. He clenched his ass to protect his hole, but I moved so he couldn't get to my cock. He got the message and opened his buns.

I did not intend to fuck him that night, but I wanted him to know the score. I sucked him some and got to taste his precum. He did the same to me. He didn't just like it, he loved it. I turned off the shower; we dried off and went to my bedroom.

We sixty-nined for a while then had to cool down. It wanted some more quality time with his cock before we traded sperm. He was afraid I was done, but I reassured him I just wanted to catch my breath. He was relieved.

"I don't know what's gotten into me," he said. "I've never done anything like this in my life."

"I was kind of guessing you hadn't enjoyed anything so much before either?"

"You're right. It was mind blowing," Dean said. "I had no idea. You're not my type at all."

I laughed. "I may not be your type, but my cock is."

"You must think I'm a jerk. I'm embarrassed," he said.

"No need for that. It was good for me and good for you, so who cares," I said. "I've known some guys who get really turned on by big meat. They weren't gay. They just responded to donkey dongs."

"Does that offend you?"

"Not one bit," I replied. "It's kind of flattering." I leaned over and sucked his some more. He was hard as a rock. "Let me try something a little different." I said.

I straddled him, positioned his cock at my ass and sat on it. It was a good fit. The pressure on my prostate was good and got me even harder. I wiggled some on his cock and he stroked mine. He was in heaven. I figured he'd like it. In this position, He both got to fuck me and play with my cock. It was the perfect arrangement for a macho, cock hungry man.

I think it was safe to say Dean was in heaven. He shot off in my ass as I popped. My seed coated his torso and he took it well. We broke apart after the ejaculations stopped and showered again. Much to my surprise Dean got in bed with me and we talked. The conversations were mostly about the case, but I had expected him to high tail it out of my apartment.

After a while, his hand strayed back to my cock and we had a second suck session. His interest in my cock had not diminished one bit. When he shot off, I lapped it up. As often is the case, his orgasm induced me to shoot too. I warned him I was going to blow, but he stayed sucking my knob and got a mouthful. I think he did it just to be polite, but he really seemed to enjoy it.

It took a lot for Dean to swallow a mouthful of redneck cum, but he did it. Of course, I had an ass full of cop cum, so it all evened out, but he did well. He went home. I knew he'd be back.

The next day was our big rehearsal day. Our big scenes, the one in which Bottom changes into an ass and the Pyramis and Thisbe play itself needed final rehearsals before we were melded into the whole play.

My vision of acting was deeply flawed. I thought you learned your lines and then just said them. Maybe some actors do that, but Charlie, the director, and a vision for the play that included every movement and every facial expression. I was a small cog in a complicated mechanism he controlled.

One of two of the actors balked, but as far as I could tell, they weren't the best actors. Fred, who had double if not triple the experience of the rest of the crew didn't seem to worry one bit. He had played Bottom several times before and knew the words. Fortunately as the low man on the totem pole, I was to baldly recite my lines as if I had barely memorized them. Charlie thought my accent and the costume would do the rest.

The love scene between Bottom and Titania was a wild romp. Samuel played Titania and was just under four feet tall. Fred, who played Bottom was six four. Samuel did well, very well. He played the smitten Queen of the Fairies with flair and grace. I knew he had spent some time doing the dance of love on Fred's pole. Samuel liked the bottom and Bottom the top.

Robert remained bitter and a bit uninvolved. The two men playing Helena and Hermia had come around. I think they knew if they didn't get their act together, they would have been totally upstaged by Samuel's Titania. Lance, who played Hippolyta was pretty in drag and played it straight. In the battle between the gay Queens, Samuel won hands down, but Helena and Hermia acquitted themselves well.

All the dwarfs were there to give support to Samuel. He was the youngest of the group. Charlie actually took advice from David and Rudy. They were experienced actors who were helpful working out the full sized person and dwarf relationships. After about three hours, things were going well.

Theseus had just said, "Your play need no excuse," when the theater was rocked by a huge bang. I knew immediately it was an explosion. A second later smoke poured in from the front lobbies and the fire alarms when off.

I had some experience with bombs and I knew this was much smaller than the explosion that blew up part of the city a few years earlier. There was a lot of smoke, but the emergency lights went on and for a group of what I thought were rather flighty actors, we evacuated the building quickly going into the rear alley. There was no panic. I went around to the front of the building. The main doors were blown out, but the rest of the front was fine. Smoke was pouring out of the doors, but there was no flame.

The city Fire Department was there in what seemed liked seconds, as were the Police. The Fire Department had suffered badly in the earlier disaster and I noted they established an HQ away from the site. The former Chief died in the one of the secondary explosions at the Temple Bombing. Rescue trucks were everywhere, and I saw some ATF cars. Charlie was hyper organized and had done a head count of the cast and crew. Everyone was accounted for.

I thought the media was slow arriving, but two local channels had eyes in the sky nearby so there was live broadcast on the local stations. John, who was playing Theseus, was there to give an eyewitness account. He gave a low key and reassuring report. He lived near the Temple and had been home when that bomb blew. John was the television morning man and was associated with snow closings and he been on air for 36 hours during the last hurricane. He was nothing if not unflappable and reasonable. He won an award for his hurricane coverage.

"It struck me as a small device," he said. "It certainly could have hurt someone, but it was nothing like the Temple bomb."

"That was set off by terrorists," the woman interviewing him asked, "Do you think this is the work of foreign terrorist?"

"The Temple bomb was set off by home grown terrorist, not foreigners," John said firmly. "As a general rule, I don't think terrorists are into theater much. If I had to hazard a guess, I would say either this is an accidental explosion, like a can of solvent, or it was a prank that got out of hand.  Of course there is the possibility of a drama critic gone wild, but the play hasn't open yet."

At that point, Fred walked by in his Bottom costume, wearing a huge ass head.  He gave the interview in costume and made quite a splash on the evening news programs.  In the strange way that the world works, the next day we had an outbreak of advanced ticket sales.

That night the bomb squad confirmed it was indeed a bomb, not an accidental explosion.  It was a pipe bomb and a Molotov cocktail taped together, but the bomb maker had used Diesel fuel, rather than gasoline.  The Diesel smoked and eventually burned, but it did not explode.  The bomb had been set in the Ladies' restroom.  The bomb squad found fingerprints on the Molotov cocktail.  That was a shock to me.

It was strictly Amateur Night.  Of course this was an all-male production with the only women in the play were working the lights and helping with some of the costuming and scenery.  The bomb squad assumed the person setting the bomb didn't want to hurt anyone.

The bombing struck me as a poor choice, given the city's recent history with bombing.  If you wanted to touch a raw nerve, a bomb was a sure fire way to do it.  Neither the Fire Department, nor the Police Department were prone to be open minded about bombing.  The objective might have been to touch the raw nerve.  I struck me the bomber might not have been aware of the eight year old bombing of the Temple, or was a space cadet who didn't realize the significance.  I thought about Eldon's votaries.

My office's computer nerds went after the bomb and found the recipe on the net.  Actually, they did better than that.  They found the original recipe and the incorrect recipe the bomb maker used.  The original recipe was from a French Anarchist site.  Someone translated gasoline as petrol and our bomb maker assumed it was any petrol, not just gasoline. That was what I thought. One of my friends pointed out a big truck stop north of Richmond was named Petrol. They had closed circuit television on the pumps at all times. The Richmond police got the tapes and went over them. That bore fruit eventually.

Dean came over to see me that night. I was with David and Rudy. We were having a beer and going over the day's events. He was uneasy with the dwarfs there, but I told him they were all right. "Let me go through this with you," Dean said after I gave him a beer. "We have poison pen letters, slashed tires and a suspicious man following a cast member back from a rehearsal. Then Maurice dies in a fall, and now we have a bombing. Is there any possible way these items can't be related?"

"It seems likely to me, but there is a problem with modus operandi," I said.

"Would a poison pen letter writer set off a bomb?" David asked. "Letter writing is passive, long distance, hands-off aggression. Pushing Maurice down the stairs was anything but hands off."

"Someone or some persons are twisted," Rudy said. "There is lots of jealousy and envy among actors, but almost no violence. We tend to act, but not do."

"Perhaps there is a director and several actors involved?" I suggested.

"If this were a play it would be shitty. It's confused and incoherent," Dean remarked. "Who would put on a play like that?"

"The number of crappy plays is stunning," David said. "Good directors aren't that common either. I can't tell you how many plays I've been to that were supposed to the greatest play since Hamlet, that were total failures."

"Every year there are multimillion dollar productions on Broadway done by hot-shot producers that fail miserably."

"So we're looking for a shitty play directed by an inept hot shot?" Dean asked.

"One more thing, the worst plays are written by directors," Rudy said.

"How common are these no talent schmucks?" Dean asked.

"A dime a dozen," David said. We continued discussing the alternatives. Dean went to the bathroom and David followed. Rudy and I were still chatting when David poked his head out of the bath and gestured at us to join him. I hadn't noticed the water was running in the shower.

Dean had discovered the joys of dwarf sex. David and Rudy were engaging men, very masculine, cheerful and sexually driven. They weren't shy. David was the master of the sneak attack. When you run into a fully-grown man who is less than four feet tall the last thing in the world you expect is for him to make a pass at you. David pointed out, he never had face-to-face conversations, and it is always face to crotch. "That normally can be a problem, but in the shower it's a blessing," he said. "There I'm face to cock, and the cock is my favorite organ. As luck would have it, it's just about every man's favorite organ."

David and Rudy aren't intimidating and you tend to think of them as a curiosity more than as sex partners. By the time you realized they were fully equipped sexual men, they might already be in your ass, using their cocks to massage your prostate. I think that's want happened to Dean. By the time he satisfied his curiosity, he was fully sexually engaged.

When Rudy and I joined them, Dean was relaxed and having a great time. We frolicked in the shower and then went to my bed. Rudy was into anal big time and Dean helped him with that. He was poking Rudy doggy style when he opened his own hole. David couldn't resist the temptation. Dean jerked a little when he felt the lubricated cock head as his asshole, but he didn't stop fucking Rudy. David had six and a half thick inches of meat and it slid into Dean's ass like a heated knife into butter.

Dean later told me it was the first time he had been fucked. He must have been hyper receptive, since it's rarely that easy. Dean only lasted a minute or two, and then he popped.

They broke apart, and then David fucked me. His cock felt good, but not so good I was going to shoot. We had a nice long session until David finally popped. At this point, Rudy rejoined me and sat on my cock. As I said, both David and Rudy were full size men above the legs, but it was still a surprise when my cock fit in Rudy's body.

Dean had been watching this through a drowsy post orgasmic haze. The second he realized I was going to fuck Rudy he was fully alert. His cock, that had been resting, came back to life. My cock was still magic for him.

# Part 6

Sometimes the most casual, lust filled event can bear fruit. After Dean and the dwarfs left, I got a call from Rufus. He needed to talk, right away he said. I told him to come over early the next morning. I was afraid he was having guilt pangs about his trip on the wild side.

"How early?" he asked.

"I'm up at six," I said.

Rufus arrived at 6:30 with another young man named Temple. Temple was older and bigger than Rufus and knew who I was. He told Rufus the actor-portraying wall was in fact, Clydesdale, the detective. Rufus knew something and he was afraid.

"I think I'm in trouble," Rufus said. "Temple and I were talking about the bomb at the theater. I think I know something about it."

"Tell me what you know," I said. "I can tell you if you're in trouble."

"I don't want to rat on a friend," he said.

"Ratting on a friend has to do with a baseball breaking a neighbor's window," I replied. "We are talking big time felonies here. Bombings and murder."

"Murder?" Rufus said, obviously shocked. Then it dawned on him. "That costume maker?" I nodded.

"Temple lived in the Fan District near the Temple. I was thinking the bomb was a joke. He says it isn't," Rufus said.

"My neighbor's house was burned out. My little brother was cut by flying glass," Temple said. "Bombs aren't jokes."

"They actually didn't use the words bomb. They said Midsummer would go out with a bang, with a great big bang," Rufus said.

"Okay, who are they?"

"Emma and her pal Eileen were talking. Eileen is writing a play on Russian anarchists and was doing research on home-made bombs," Rufus said. "They were talking about how easy it was to make a bomb. They were talking about making a little list."

"Eileen was in a production of the Mikado when she was in school," Temple added. "She played one of the three little school girls, but was really bitter about not getting the Lord High Executioner role."

"Who played the Lord High Executioner?" I asked.

"I did," Temple said. "I'm a bass-baritone."

"Are you a Drama major?"

"Nope, I was a music major, specializing in choral directing," Temple said. "I am the associate director of music for Wally." Wally was an old friend and playmate of mine. Wally ran a tight ship, and if Temple was his associate, Temple was okay.

"Eileen is 100% bitch, mean nasty and rude. She has a chip on her shoulder as big as Mount Rushmore," Temple said. "She never fails to get a part; she is screwed out of it. Every one of her performances is perfect, if she only hadn't been sabotaged by the no talent drones she's force to work with."

"Miss Sunshine?" I asked. Both Rufus and Temple laughed. "Getting back to business, why are they doing this? What could justify a bomb?"

"Eileen hates Shakespeare. She one of those types who thinks we need to discard the old so new can bloom. She says it why real plays are so rare today." Rufus said. "Emma is a follower and has no mind of her own. She just does what Eileen or Eldon tells her."

"Is Eileen associated with Eldon?"

"Just professionally," Rufus said.

"They sleep together," Temple said.

"You're kidding!" Rufus exclaimed.

"Of course I am not. Eldon use to fuck her two or three times a week just after rehearsals. They never slept." Temple said. "I had the apartment next to her for a year. Eldon was a regular visitor."

"They fucked?" Rufus asked in disbelief.

"The walls were thin. "Get it deeper, deeper, deeper!" was the phrase I heard," Temple said. "I don't think they were planting Tulips."

"Eileen did not get in the all-female Macbeth, and she regards the all-male Midsummer as a gay plot," Rufus said. "She has relationship problems with men. She thinks it because her potential mates are lured away by the glamour of the gay life style."

"Was she at Byrd when they had the earlier poison pen event?" I asked. Rufus knew nothing of the earlier outbreak, but Temple knew about it.

"I'm not positive, but she could have been," he said. "I got one of the letters."

"I thought it was a Theater Department thing?" I said.

"That was while I was playing the Lord High Executioner. My letter suggested I got the part by blowing the director and I had kept the part from going to a real man," Temple said. "It was completely untrue. I fucked the director a year and a half after the last performance." We laughed.

"How were the reviews?" Rufus asked.

"They were glowing. We had to add extra performances," Temple said. "I was listed as an up and coming musical comedy star. "A gifted actor with a beautiful and expressive voice," were the exact words they used, not that I remember the exact words."

"Was this before or after the ill-fated Hamlet?" I asked.

"Just before," Temple said, "As I recall Eldon referred to it as drivel for the plebeians. Tony was always gracious to other plays and directors."

"Did either woman mention Eldon with respect to the big bang?" I asked.

"No, not at all," Rufus said. "There is one odd thing. Emma asked me where she could get some petrol. I asked if she meant gasoline. Petrol is what the English call gas. She said she needed petrol. I told her to go to the Petrol station. She looked it up in the yellow pages and found a Petrol Station."

That is what they call a clue. Rufus had to leave. He had a job. Temple stayed.

"Wally said I'd like you," he said. "Actually, he said I'd really like you."

"Are you a size queen?"

"I think it would be more correct to say I aspire to be a size queen," Temple said.

"Bottom?"

"God yes!" he replied.

"I need to take a shower. Do you want to join me?"

Temple started to take off his shirt. I took that as a yes. He was naked by the time I got the water going. He over six feet tall and looked as if he still had his baby fat. Temple would need to be careful about his weight as he got older. Curly black hair covered his body and his cock was more than respectable. He was a solid seven inches and had bull balls. It took about two or three seconds to realize he was a first rate cock sucker.

He didn't look it, but his father must have been a snake. He must have had one of those detachable jaws that let snakes swallow things three times their size. We had a quick shower so we could get on the bed and 69.

Being enthusiastic and appreciative is a nice characteristic for a man, and Temple was that. He liked my cock and wasn't afraid to show it. I got into him big time too. When I deep throated him I suctioned great globs of precum from his balls. He was ripe and ready. When I buried my nose into his balls I smelled the musky scent of man, but also caught a whiff of lubricant. His ass was already lubricated. That too is a clue to what he wanted.

He wanted to get fucked from the rear. I got him on his side and wedged my cock between his buns. Temple was no virgin and he had a realistic sense of what it would take to get my entire cock in his ass. He was willing to do what he needed to do. It took a while, but both he and I were happy with the results. The first half of my cock was hard for him to take, but the second half was fine. I was hitting spots in his ass never before touched by a cock.

Sometimes I wonder if there is ever a point when you can say you've done it all sexually. It seems to me there are always new experiences. Sometimes it's due to a new partner or situation. Temple was young and had hardly scratched the surface. I'm not so young and feel the same. I've been surprised when I was with an old friend or playmate like John the contractor or Wally the organist, and we end up in a new place. I don't know how many times I've fucked them, and it's new more often than not.

Once I got Temple fully impaled and I kept the pressure up until he shot. I pulled out and let him rest, and then went in from the front. That position on his back with his legs on my shoulders leaves me in the driver's seat. I get to watch his face and cock and see him react.

He had already shot off so I wasn't sure how good the refill would be for him. As my cock slid into his hole, Temple's cock inflated. It was as if my cock was pumping it full. I guess in a sense it was. Temple ass was a wonder and it seemed to accommodate my cock easily. We had ten or fifteen minutes of fun then he popped a second time and I shot off too. We showered again the day was well started. I called Dean and told him what I had found out.

This was to be a long day. Crews were cleaning and repairing the theater, so it was a mad house. A number of students and volunteers appeared to clean up the scenery. My friend Bobby Wilmot came to help and I asked him to take attendance. I was interested in who might show up. Bobby was a fixture of Richmond Theater life and he provided coffee and refreshments for the cleaning crew. He was also a confirmed gossip and no one would think it was odd if he was asking questions.

We were to have a photo shoot of the costumes and scenes. These were used for publicity and for the actors' resumes. Once the performances were over, this would be the only visual record of the play, so the actors needed good pictures. While I didn't have much of a future as an actor, I was in a number of scenes and I had to be there to complete the ensemble. My costume had turned out well and Skyler wanted good photos.

We went to the William Byrd University Theater for the photos. It was between plays and was big enough to stage the photos with a black background. The actual scenery was being cleaned and freshened up. The Duke of Richmond's Players was independent of the university, but there was a close informal relationship.

The photo shoot took forever. The photographer was good and Charley wanted the pictures to be atmospheric. A rather aggressive woman named Liz was the photographer. She was no nonsense, but had a clear vision of what Charley wanted. She had two helpers to do the lights and set up. One was a slim bearded guy named Carl, and the other was a nerdy guy they called Stoner. He had a slightly ZZ Top like look, but was good with the lights.

Carl helped with the costumes, since most of the dressers were working at the theater. He was business like with my peasant costume, but when I changed to my wall costume, Carl was less business like. I couldn't get into my costume without being completely naked. It was an all-male cast, so that wasn't a problem. For Carl it was an opportunity. I needed help getting some of the straps that held it together attached. I was the last one in the dressing room. I told him I needed some help. He said he'd help, but had to do something first. He disappeared for a few seconds and returned with Stoner. Carl was helpful. Skyler had been strictly business when he dressed me. Stoner was strictly funny business.

"Damn, is that fucker real?" he whispered to me. That was a rhetorical question. He had my cock in his hand. "Damn, it's a beauty."

"You like them big?"

"I sure do," Stoner replied. "Do you give samples?" He was like a kid asking a star for an autograph. If I weren't always horny I'd have told him to buzz off. Stoner had all the sophistication of a construction boot, but I kind of liked the direct approach.

"I have my heart set on not getting my pictures taken without a hard on," I said. "Maybe after the shoot?"

"I have hit the jack pot today!" Stoner exclaimed. "I live nearby. I'll wait for you after the shoot." I finished getting dressed and went to get my picture taken.

I hadn't shaved in two weeks so my face was a furry as my body. Carl had fluffed up my chest, back and belly hair so it merged with the ivy and the primroses Skyler had woven into the costume. If anything shifted and inch or two I would have a problem with indecent exposure. I soon realized that wasn't going to happen. Skyler was a craftsman and everything stayed in place and was surprisingly comfortable too.

The photographer, Liz, had a good time. We were the last shoot and she was fast. Liz did film and digital pictures. I saw the digitals and they were good. I looked spectacular. It looked like an unruly patch of second growth. If you knew who I was you could tell it was me, but otherwise I was transformed. After the shoot, I got out of my costume and went home with Stoner.

Stoner lived in a hippie pad a few blocks from the university. He wasn't old enough to have been a hippie, but he must have liked the look. Given the combinations of beads, tie died fabrics and Lava lamps. I immediately noticed the absence of the smell of marijuana. I mentioned that and Stoner told me that was all in his past.

"You've had some problems?"

"That's one way to put it," Stoner replied. "I had the worst case of self-hating fag known to man. Carl straightened me out." As if on cue, Carl came in the front door of the apartment.

"Damn it Stoner, you're mellowing. I thought you'd be naked by now," Carl said. "Stoner's the romantic type. Every once and a while he looks at the face of the guy he's sleeping with."

"I'm the romantic type too," I said. "I like to get down to business and then talk afterwards."

"Do you mind if I watch?" Carl asked.

"As long as you get naked, it's fine," I said. "I like threesomes too." By then Stoner was taking off his shirt. We went to the bedroom. They were an oddly miss matched pair. Both were tall and thin, Carl worked out, but Stoner wasn't in bad shape. Both were hairy. Carl had pitch black hair and while his chest, gut and back were hairy it looked as if every hair was manicured. Stoner was dirty blond and it looked like he had been tumble dried and had no access to a comb. He had that look some dogs get when they really need to go to a groomer.

I soon realized they were a team. While Stoner was the most vocal in his admiration of my cock, but I think I really turned on Carl. Stoner was also a bit shy, unlike Carl. We had a good time. Much to my amazement, it was Carl who took a ride on my cock. Not only did he ride it, he did a convincing imitation of a cowboy on a bucking bronco.

Stoner wanted my cock but was timid. I took my time and it turned out to be fine. I slipped in his rear as we relaxed on the bed. It was slow and gradual. Carl spiced it up by rear-ending me. He had a long thin member and it was nice and easy. Eventually we traded places and I fucked Carl a second time as Stoner screwed me. That was the highlight of the afternoon.

Carl was open and my cock slid in easily, then he'd tighten his sphincter and held me in. Stoner had a fat, meaty cock and it did a job on my prostate. We were all excited and turned on. Stoner was a lovely fucker. He made love to my asshole, no mean feat. I noticed he produced a lot of pre cum, so when he was in my ass he was self-lubricating. He had a tendency to have single shot ejaculations rather than a single orgasm. We had an impressive triple orgasm and rested. We talked.

They were William Byrd University graduates and had been together for six years. They had been at William Byrd University during the previous poison pen episode and Stoner had been the light man for Hamlet.

"You know, the only thing the critic from the newspaper liked about the play was the lighting," Stoner said. "If you want to learn how to lose friends, let that happen to you. Eldon hasn't spoken to me since."

"What I hear about Eldon makes me think he's a special guy," I said.

"Special is one way to put it," Stoner said. "Have you ever seen the movie, The Prime of Miss Jean Brodie?"

"A long time ago."

"Well I was impressed by Eldon when he came here, then I saw the movie. Miss Jean Brodie was a teacher who lived through her students. She got them to do what she was too timid to do," Stoner explained. "That is Eldon. He leads you on and gets you to take risks he's unwilling to do. He's the big time radical, but you get to be stuck in a disaster of a play in front of half the town and all your friends. He walks away and says the actors were too immature to carry out his high concept. It was the concept that ate shit, not the actors."

"Do you know Emma and Eileen?" I asked.

Carl rolled his eyes. "Emma is just pathetic; Eileen would have been well suited to be a nurse at Auschwitz. They are two stupid women."

"Talk about the Miss Jean Brodie problem!" Stoner exclaimed. "Ninety percent of the students who fell under Eldon's spell out grew it. Not them. They both think he's Jesus here for the second coming and Studly Do Right too."

"Could they have been part of the antigay letters writing campaign?"

"Shit, I could have been part of that campaign," Stoner said. "Eldon was into real men, and that's what I wanted to be, not a gay guy. I can barely write a word. If I sent the letter, the recipients would be complaining more about the spelling than the contents of the letter. I'm a lot better hating myself than hating other people."

"What made you see the light?"

"Carl. I had no idea anyone as handsome and talented as Carl could love me," Stoner said.

"You're overstating it again," Carl said.

# Part 7

The case was moving along at a good pace.  I called Dean with the information I got from Rufus, Carl and Stoner.  Dean was good and had the resources to get a lot of the legwork done.  Emma was in the cross hairs.

Dean called me the next morning.  Emma had fallen off the balcony of her apartment.  She wasn't technically dead, but that was a mere technicality.  There was massive brain damage and a broken back.  There was no doubt in my mind that Emma was in this sordid affair up to her eyeballs.  She was stupid and delusional.

There also was no doubt in my mind that she was not the brains behind the scheme.  Emma wasn't a leader; she was a spear-carrier, not a lead.  Being stupid and delusional doesn't deserve the death penalty.

Up until this event, it was possible to consider the poison pen letters as an effort to sabotage the play.  There was jealousy of another director's success and the perpetrators apparently had no grip on reality. The possible success of Midsummer's Night Dream would reflect badly on the failure of Hamlet. While the persons involved wouldn't admit it to themselves, Midsummer was going well.

This all could be interpreted as a nasty prank gone bad or just extraordinarily over the top. That made sense given the personalities of the people involved. Maurice's death could have been accidental, manslaughter rather than murder. I could visualize Maurice coming on someone doing something in the wrong place. There might have been a struggle and Maurice fell.

Emma couldn't be an accident. Emma had been sloppy and obvious. She knew who was behind the scheme. Nothing about my brief encounter with Emma suggested she would hold up to serious police style interrogation. No, she wouldn't squeal on her friends, but she would get tripped up on a simple question. She would make a slip and all would come out. She might not realize the true import of what she knew. I doubted she would have been involved in Maurice's death, but she might have known who was at the theater that night.

Rufus called me just after I heard of Emma's fall. He knew the full import. I told him he needed to call Dean and ask to give a full statement on the record. This was too serious to let informal exchanges of information. I also gave him the name of a Lawyer friend of mine who might be able to help.

I went to the theater. I had a man prowling the area, but I also noted two police undercover agents in the area too. Inside the theater there was the smell of fresh paint, and a very slight reminder of smoke, but all was well. The cleaning and repair crews had done a good job. We were to do a full run through of the play with costumes, scenery, music and lighting to get the technical stuff right. Dress rehearsal was the next night and opening night on the next day. Everyone was keyed up and excited.

I had one of my men serving as a janitor in the front lobby and another back stage. There were a number of people in the audience. These were all friends of the actors or staff. Stoner was working with the lights. Carl was in the balcony with a video camera. He was taping the performance.

Charlie was nothing if not anal-retentive. He wanted to see what it looked like from all areas. They provided instant replay of potential problems in the play. I could feel the tenseness, but there was a strong "the play must go on" feel too.

The first scenes went on without a hitch. They were the boring part of the play as far as I could tell. Our first scene went well. The costumes for this were simple and it was mostly a strong performance by Fred as Bottom. The fairies did very well. The dwarfs were surprisingly effective, even Samuel as Titania. He played it straight, imperious and willful.

There were several screw-ups in the lighting and a dry ice problem for the fairy scenes. These were quickly resolved. I was a problem, or more correctly, my costume was. It was a lot of work to change from my peasant garb into my wall costume. Skyler was there to help. I was the least important of the characters in the play, but Charlie wanted every character to play his part. I was at the center of the play within the play at the end. That the wall got a laugh was important.

The chink in the wall, that was at the core of the Pyramis and Thisbe story, was at my crotch and the risqué peaking through the chink was a typical Shakespearean off color joke. It came off flawlessly. The stage crew was laughing. Fred was spectacular as Bottom, and the play ended on a high note.

The bomb had focused attention on the play in the city, and publicity was building. There was a comment in the paper that the play might well be exceptionally clever. The publicity photographs were out. They featured Fred in his ass head and me as Tom Snout, the wall. I wasn't recognizable. Since I was almost nude I was memorable. As a group, we mechanicals looked like a body hair fetishist's convention. I was described as a furry creature with a severe outbreak of ivy.

Dean was in the audience and saw me afterward. "It may sound stupid, but you were good," he said. "It may have been a small role, but you stood out."

"What was your impression of the whole thing?" I asked.

"I've never got Shakespeare before, but this was good," he said. "I understood it. Lots of laughs, funny lines. It a pretty show too. It took me ten minutes to get into it and then it took off."

"How do you think our whack job will take it?"

"My guess he or she would rather eat broken glass than see this succeed," Dean said. "We're going to have high security for the next few nights. There's not much time to make a move. My main worry is for the individual actors."

"That may not be a problem. Skyler told me he's warned everyone they should not go out alone, and to stay near friends," I said. "That's where the audience came from today. Henry thought that was foolish, but Skyler doesn't take no for an answer. He called Henry's wife and she called his folks. They are here. His mom is baby-sitting, his dad is watching."

"Was that the beefy man to the side of row three?"

"The man who looks like a professional wrestler?" I asked. Dean nodded. "That was papa. He looks like a one-man demolition company. No one is going to get near to Henry. Charlie's partner was there too. He runs a gym."

After the rehearsal, I got a message from Dean on my cell phone. Emma was officially brain dead and her parents were coming to decide what to do. I had another message from Rufus. He had run into Eldon and Eileen at a restaurant, and they seemed to be having a celebration of some sort.

Liz the photographer came over to me. "I hate to impose of you, but I teach a photography class at night and I would love to use you as a model. You present a challenge," she said.

"A lot of people think I'm a challenge, even my mother sometimes," I said.

She laughed, "That's not what I meant. The hairy body and the ivy present a challenge in focusing," she explained. "You could give the autofocus a run for its money. You are already in costume; it would only be for an hour."

"Now?"

"If you could do it," she said.

"Did your regular model just call in sick?"

Liz looked shocked. "Damn, Charlie said you were smarter than you look."

"That doesn't take much," I said. "If you're in pinch, I'll do it,"

"Charlie said you were a good sport too," Liz added. She had her van nearby. I put a raincoat over the foliage and got to the studio in the University's art building. It was a class of 15 or 18 men and women. About half were undergraduates, but the remainder was older.

They were a bit shocked when I appeared. The regular model was a pretty young woman, but they adapted quickly. As I would have guessed, Liz had the shoot well organized. She would set up lights for a particular effect. There would be a ten-minute shooting session, and then she would reset the lights. She did soft indirect light, strong shadows, back lighting etc.

The students had to work quickly. Most had a digital, a traditional camera either black and white, color, or both. A few of the students weren't into it at all, but they were the exception. By the time we reached the third pose, most had figured out what worked and were having a good time. At the end, Liz asked if I could stay for a final longer pose. I said I would.

"Class, if you wish to stay our model will stay for a final pose. This pose will be up to you and you will have more time. This will give you an opportunity to use what you have discovered in the first four poses," she said.

The dead wood left the studio. One girl apologized she couldn't stay; she had a ride she had to catch. Now that the students were use to me they began to talk mostly about Midsummer's Night Dream as they worked. They knew all about the poison pen letters and the one of the older students knew about the earlier incident.

They also knew there was something fishy about Emma's death. "I heard she was the letter writer," one student said.

"She may have written them, but I bet she was taking dictation," the student who knew of the earlier incident, said, "I had a date with the Wicked Witch of 32nd Street when I was an undergraduate. She wrote the letters."

"Who in hell was the Wicked Witch of 32nd Street?" a younger student asked.

"Eileen Miller. She was here during the earlier incident. She and Emma were thick as thieves. Back then, she was pretty and willing to put out. That was really important to me at the time. I was 20 and she was an older woman of 24," he said. "Once the sex was over things went downhill rapidly. Men were the cause of all evil. They were either fags, or they betrayed her; they cheated her, they used her and then through her away. She was a bitter woman who couldn't understand why she only got one-night stands. She actually hit me. As far as I could tell, she hated all men, not just fags. I've known men who disliked women except for the sex, but she was the first women I met who hated men, but liked their cocks.

"I thought they made dildos for that?" a man suggested.

"It ain't the same!" Liz replied.

"She never found true love, I take it?" a younger girl asked.

"She found true love alright. She found Mephistopheles for her Faust. She told me about him. He was a director of some sort, and a genius, an unrecognized genius if you get my drift.

"That must be Eldon," Liz said. "No one can recognize his genius because there isn't any. He moves with an entourage. Emma and Eileen were the leaders, a few impressionable undergraduates and Fenton."

"Who is Fenton? I know about the others," the older student asked.

"He's a sad case. He took a course from me, but he knew it all. He was un teachable. I tried to get him to get some counseling, but I don't think he did." Liz said. "At the end of the semester he scared me."

"Damn it Liz, I thought you could scare away the abominable snowman?"

"Normally, I can," she said. "He failed to turn in his final project for the semester so he got an automatic failing grade. He sent me a letter saying I was unworthy of teaching a student of his talents."

Liz's cell phone rang.  From her conversation, it was obviously about a sick child at home.

"I have to get home.  Do any of you need a ride? You know my rule; no one walks home alone.  Ladies, pack up your cameras.  Gentlemen, you can close up the room when you are done?"

"Of course, Liz," the older man said.  "Is it Robin again?" Liz nodded.

"Oh, I have our favorite Wall's clothes in the bag in the corner. Someone is going to need to help him get out of the ivy.  Make sure you don't damage it, or Wall for that matter," Liz said.

"Don't worry, we've got it covered," the older man said.  "You take care of Robin.  We'll take care of the Wall."

Liz and all the students except for two left.  "Liz's daughter has leukemia; it's an iffy situation," the older man explained.  "I'm Steve by the way.  This is Slim," he said as he introduced the remaining man.

"I'm Clydesdale," I said.  "Taking this thing off isn't easy.  I have my own dresser."

"I'm a fashion design student," Slim said.  "There ain't anything I can't take off and put back together again." I knew the basic arrangement of the costume, but had no idea what was attached behind my back. The costume wasn't fragile, but it wasn't made for mountain climbing either.

It took about ten or fifteen minutes of work, but I got out of it and all the parts were intact.  I was so worried the costume would get damaged; I hadn't noticed I was naked in front of the two men.  They, however, noticed me.

"Damn, surprises never cease," Slim said when he saw my cock.

Steve laughed. "Slim's not the refined type. He's always looking for love in all the wrong places. I myself would never notice that horse cock hanging between your legs."

"I have friends who claim it's not a cock. It's bait," I said.

"Does anyone swallow it hook line and sinker?" Slim asked.

"Damn Slim, I didn't know you could think that fast. That was good." Steve remarked. "I hate to put an end to this witty repartee, but is there any chance you would let us take some nude pictures? They'd be art, not porno."

"I'm naked anyway, why not," I said. "I don't really have much of a problem with porn for that matter."

"I have a sneaky suspicion the University wouldn't approve." Steve said. We had a quick photographic session then I got dressed. Steve and Slim had a dispute as to who would take me to my car. I knew what the real problem was.

"If you boys want to get me alone so you can make a pass at me, forget it. I've got no problem playing with either of you, or both of you for that matter," I said. They took me to the theater to return the costume. Skyler was still there making last minute improvements. When Slim met Skyler I saw love at first sight blossom. Slim volunteered to help Skyler and Steve and I went off to his apartment. It had been a long day, but it was only 9:30.

Steve was a high school English and Drama teacher who was adding photography to his skill set. He was not a size queen and he was a top. I asked him if he wanted me to come home with him. It didn't seem like a perfect fit.

"If I told you I haven't had any sex in six months when my partner walked out and I'm horny as shit, would you still come home with me?" he asked.

"I'm a fucking Mother Theresa when it comes to horny men," I said. "Guys have to help each other out sometimes." He said thanks and we went into his apartment. We took a shower together then went to the bedroom.

"I was trying to think, but I'm not sure I've ever been with an uncut guy before," Steve said. I sat in chair and he got down and began to nurse on my cock. At first he didn't suck it; he just played with the skin. He tongued the skin and sucked it into his mouth and then slowly worked his tongue into the pucker.

I hadn't realized how tired I was. I don't think I actually fell asleep, but I was more than willing for him to play with my foreskin without expending the energy on getting an erection. I was afraid he'd think I was rude for being so laid back, but that wasn't a problem at all. Steve wasn't a size queen, but he was in the process of discovering he was a foreskin fetishist.

Steve didn't know this. He had never sucked an uncut cock so there was no way for him to know. He also hadn't realized that one of the extras of horse cock is a wide slit. I had a wide slit and a wide cum tunnel. The pucker of the foreskin pretty well lines up with the slit. His tongue didn't just explore the warm space between the skin and my cock head; it went down the tunnel into my shaft.

The chance this would happen and I wouldn't get hard was slim but it happened. I was in the chair half-asleep. Steve was a stealth sucker. He was slow and gentle and made no sudden moves. When I came out of the half sleep, Steve was excited.

We got on the bed and sixty-nined. I got hard them, but Steve was already hooked. He was an average guy. He was of average height, slightly hairy and possessed an average cock. It was beefy but average length. His head was well defined and flared. His balls were big and he had a nice sack.

Somehow, his cock was perfect for sucking. I could easily take it all and every time I did, I suctioned precum from his balls. It twitched and once and a while I'd get a little taste of his sperm mixed in with the precum. It was intensely pleasurable and stimulating, but I didn't feel the tenseness you get when you are building up to a climax. It was low stress.

We took a rest break. "I didn't think you'd be like this at all," Steve said. "I thought I'd be trying to keep your cock out of my ass. I haven't had this much fun in years."

"I like to fuck, I don't need to fuck. Your former partner wasn't active sexually?"

"He could never quite get his act together. He never had a job for more than six months. I think he was looking for a man who could support him in the manner he would liked to have been accustomed to," Steve said. "That isn't a high school teacher's salary. I thought he was too depressed for sex. It turned out he was giving samples to potential benefactors."

I made a stab in the dark, "When was the last time you fucked a guy." I could read his mind.

"Maybe a year and a half ago," he replied. "Are you offering?"

"I guess I am," I replied. We returned to sucking for a while. I used my spit to lube his cock and then I sat on it. I don't know exactly what happened, but the cock that was perfect for sucking was damn good for fucking too. It was big enough to know I was being fucked, but easy to take, I think it must have been just right for rubbing my prostate the right way.

We switched positions so I was on my back and he got my legs on his shoulders. This gave him control and let him fuck at his own pace. Steve was hard but fair. There was no question he wanted to shoot off, but he also wanted to have some fun along the way. I knew exactly where his cock was at all times, his cock head was bigger than I thought and I could feel it. He knew exactly where my prostate was and he loved rubbing his bloated knob against it. In short, it was the perfect fuck. It took him twenty minutes before he gave me a sperm bath.

He had a total body orgasm. He shook and shivered and quivered as he shot his seed deep in my ass. He collapsed and rested. A few minutes later he was licking my foreskin again. I was tired and dozed off. When I woke, Steve was asleep with my cock in his mouth and his tongue inside the skin.

# Part 8

The next day was the dress rehearsal and was busy. I called Dean and told him about Fenton. He had the major suspects, Eldon and Eileen under surveillance. I had found out Fenton was J. Fenton Byrd IV. Curiously, he wasn't a real Byrd, the Virginia Byrds. He was a New Jersey Byrd. Apparently they had all the pretensions of the Virginia Family without any of the achievements. He had been a theater student, but hadn't graduated and was working as a night guard at a local nursing home.

Security was high for the dress rehearsal. You would have had to be crazy to try something, but there was a chance we were dealing with someone crazy. There are people who are out of control and are not responsible for their actions. Those persons are rare. There is a much better chance that our murderer was out of control only when it suited him or her.

The dress rehearsal and the opening night were the tests to determine if the criminal was insane, or calculating. This is the way Dean saw it too. Dean told me Rufus had been helpful and was off the hook as far as criminal liability was concerned. He said, "Rufus filled in a lot of gaps. Most of it wasn't criminal or incriminating, but it did establish an atmosphere and environment. It could easily have been a prank gone bad."

"Someone took it too far?"

"That's the way I see it. It is like those fantasy games boys like. For 99% of them it's just a game, but once and a while, someone loses the boundary between fantasy and reality," Dean said. "The pranks were nasty, and the poison pen letters were illegal, but that all would have resulted in probation at worst for anyone who got caught."

"There are worse things than criminal liability," I said. "If you were an academic, or a director who got caught, exposure would end your career. You'd never work in the field again. The nastiness of the thing makes me suspect jealousy. Someone is thinking, "If I can't be a success, you can't either. That could explain some of this mess, but again, it got out of control. Perhaps the mastermind is okay, but the spear-carriers don't know the limits. Several people have mentioned actors who hated taking a bit role, and couldn't play the part without trying to over so it."

"Like someone playing the wall in Midsummer's Night Dream?"

I laughed. "I had three or four lines and that is the absolute upper limit of my acting ability and ambition. There is no Hamlet in my future."

"Well you're good semi-naked," Dean added. "Come to think about it, you're even better naked!"

"Everyone's a critic," I said as I hung up. I went to the theater. Given the hours we had spent in rehearsal, it was panicky and tense there.

Rather oddly, Skyler was a rock of calm. He was ready. He recruited a volunteer dresser to help me get into my costume. Henry's Dad, the guy who looked like a professional wrestler, was to help me. Hank had been opposed to his son's acting career, but he loved his son and was protective. He had been a college level wrestler and had stayed in shape. He had retired as the president of a wrecking company.

Skyler explained how the costume worked and what needed to be attached to make sure I didn't put on a real show for the audience. We had a few practice runs and Hank was a fast learner. In demolition it's important to get everything done in the right order. Hank understood that. He also had a good memory for faces and soon knew who was supposed to be in the dressing rooms. Skyler wouldn't scare anyone. Hank was a mountain of a man.

The dress rehearsal went well. I thought it was perfect, but Charlie saw room for improvements. I was surprised when we had a full audience for the rehearsal. They laughed at all the right places, and were enthusiastic throughout. The all-male cast wasn't like a drag show at all. Samuel was rather lovely in an imperious way as Titania. His scene with Freddy was spectacular. It was both affecting and rolling in the aisles funny.

When I appeared as the wall, there was applause. Skyler's costume was a wonder. I got more applause in the curtain calls than I would have expected. The next day several actors were to come back for a few minor modifications to fix a glitch or two in the production, but the rest of us were off until five. Fred and I had to stay late for some publicity shots for the newspapers and a television station. When I got free, Hank was waiting to help me get out of the costume.

Hank had seen me up close and personal and very naked several times as he dressed me. His wife had taken Henry and his family out to dinner after the rehearsal and Hank was alone with me. I am 100% positive Hank wasn't gay, but he was curious.

"You aren't very shy, are you?" he asked.

"What makes you think that?" I replied. Then I smiled. "I had an uncle who told me I was well equipped to be the most popular guy in a nudist camp."

Hank laughed. "I guess if I was hung like you I'd show it off too."

"It is an ice breaker," I said. "The problem is the rest of me. Not everyone is turned on by a guy who's hairy as a chimpanzee."

"My wife use to make me shave," he said. "Damn that was itchy."

"Is she used to you now?"

"Too old to care," Hank said with a tinge of disappointment in his voice. I was naked by now, but didn't make a move to get dressed. He continued. "You're uncut too. She doesn't like that much too."

"I've got some pals who like it."

"You're gay?" he asked.

"One hundred percent!"

"I bet your dance card is filled every night," he said. I moved and his hand brushed against my cock. "I admit I'm curious," he mumbled.

"I need to get home and have a sandwich. Would you like to join me?" I asked. He nodded and fifteen minutes later we were at my apartment. We had a beer and I made a couple of ham and cheese sandwiches and then we got down to business.

I told him if we were going to do a show and tell, he had to get naked too. He was all right with that. He apologized for his cock. It was normal as far as I could tell. Hank's body wasn't. He worked out and you could tell. I guessed he didn't take steroids, so he didn't have that overinflated look. He was beautiful. His broad chest was covered in even white hair. He was a natural blond and was all pink. It's a turn on to see a man as masculine as Hank so delicately colored. He was a peaches and cream stud muffin. I reached over and touched his tits.

He moaned, and then he reached over and stroked my cock.

"You tell me what you want to do," I said. "I'm an open minded guy."

"I'm really turned on but uneasy," Hank confessed. "I'm not sure. Can I just look at it?"

I went to a chair and sat. Hank got on the floor and looked as I played with it. He fondled my balls.

"You must think I'm an ass for just looking," he said.

"You won't be the first guy who just wanted to look," I said. "This may sound strange, but the media has everyone neatly divided in the straight and gay. I'm not sure anyone is that neatly divided. I know some straight guys who are really into cock. I know of a few gay guys who fell in love with a woman, and some straight men that fell for a man. Life ain't simple."

"What if a guy falls for one particular cock?" Hank asked. I laughed. As we talked, I got harder. That did nothing to reduce its appeal. Hank stood. I leaned over and sucked his semi erect cock. I could feel the tension draining from him. Three minutes later I had a mouthful of Hank's sperm. He had been fully loaded and seemed extra creamy.

"Do I have to do that with you?" he asked sheepishly.

"Nah, it's a downer after you've popped," I said. "Would you like to watch me jerk off?"

"Shit yes!" he answered with unexpected enthusiasm. I put on a good show and he enjoyed it. My cock was coated in cock juice. Hank scooped some of it up with his fingers. He looked at the quivering jiz, and then licked his fingers clean. His cock shot a final spurt as he licked up my sperm.

"Are you okay?" I asked.

"Thank you. It was good," he replied. Hank got dressed and returned to his family. I went to bed.

The next day I was on the front page of the Flair section of the paper. I had never seen me in the stage lighting, but I was a bit more naked than I had thought, but a lot more magical. It looked as if the ivy was growing out of me, and the greenery merged with my body hair. I was listed as Willard Noland and very few would have recognized me as Clydesdale. The article was flattering about the entire production.

At ten, I got a call from my mom. She had seen the picture. Mom was pleased I had taken up theater, but annoyed I hadn't told her about it. I was told in no uncertain terms to get ticket for her and my Aunts. An hour later Aunt Ellen called with the same message. She had a ladies club that wanted to see it.

"Are you certain they might see a lot more of me than they want?" I asked.

Ellen laughed. "Your Grand Daddy died before you were born, but he wasn't called Bear Lewis for nothing. He was a wonderful man, and I hadn't guessed you had inherited the gene," Ellen said. "When we were children we went swimming at the lake. I remember a friend snidely saying he might clog up the hydro plant down the river. I thought he was manly. You seem to have gotten the Noland scrawniness, but the Lewis hairiness. That is 12 tickets I need. Remember that." I called the box office; they had tickets available.

A got a full day of work done at the office and got to the theater at five. The City police were visible, as were several of my operatives and some undercover cops.

Actors are a superstitious group and everyone was on edge. Opening night jitters combined with the bombing did not promote a calm atmosphere. The K-9 unit was there sniffing for bombs. It was reassuring that they were sniffing, but most plays don't need a sweep for bombs before the opening.

The stage door was guarded by Donnie, Skyler's most effeminate costume maker and Hank. Donnie knew everyone associated with the play, or with the theater in Richmond. They seemed to get along well. Donnie gave a brief bio of everyone who entered, complete with a list of lovers, husbands wives and casual acquaintances. He knew Eldon's entire harem and could warn Hank of any trouble. Somehow Hank had met Dean and they were pals. Hank had a police radio if there were any problems.

When the police were done and gave the theater a clean, bomb free bill of health, my bomb-sniffing pooch, Killerpoo arrived. Killerpoo was the least likely bomb sniffer imaginable. He was a Cock-a-poo and something mix. Officially, he was a therapy dog, but his real love was finding bombs. He was at a stand on the sidewalk in front of the theater promoting the Richmond Therapy Dog Association. The stand was manned by staff members of the worthy institution and two of my men. Killerpoo would watch the door.

I thought it was unlikely anyone would try another bomb, but Dean disagreed. "It is amazing how attached to a particular M.O. guys can be," he said. He was right about that. He would also have been up Shit Creek if he hadn't prepared for the eventuality.

The opening performance would have been anti-climactic if the audience had not been so into it. Our timing was thrown off a little by the applause and laughter. The concept was good and the carry though was near perfect. Nothing succeeds like success and some of the more sour members of the cast were converted to admiring Charley's directing skills.

I did just fine. The curtain calls went on for a good ten minutes. Hank got me out of my costume and I had the feeling if we had been alone he might well have taken a lick. We all went to a post-performance party at a nearby hotel. Our local critic, Milton Hammerly, was effusive in his praise, and actually apologized for his rudeness earlier. The icing on the cake was a man who turned out to be a drama critic for the Washington Post. He was doing a story on up and coming regional theater companies. He loved it.

When his article came out it was entirely about the Duke of Richmond's Company and was more than flattering. He loved the play, the costumes, and the actors. He named names. It was all an up and coming theater company could want. I knew that someone, somewhere in Richmond was not celebrating with the company.

The play was a success, but there were two murders still unsolved. Maurice and Emma were dead and while we had some good leads, we weren't close to an arrest. We had Eldon, Eileen and someone named Fenton at the top of our list.

The weekend performances were packed, and they had to add additional shows during the week. There was even an outside chance the play would make money. My mother and aunts and their friends were going to come on Thursday. Hank went home, but he said he might be back next weekend if I still needed dresser. I told him that would be great. Skyler could pinch hit during the week. I wasn't a star, but the costume was. It became the most memorable image of the performance except for Fred's ass head.

On Tuesday, Milton Hammerly's housekeeper discovered him dead in the living room, the victim of a botched robbery. Dean called me with this information. Dean found a message on his answering machine from Milton from Monday night saying he needed to talk. Dean was out of the office and didn't get the message until too late. This was definitely not good.

Maybe Milton just happened to call the detective in charge of the case, and then was killed by a random burglar, but that seemed to be way too coincidental. He had found out something. There was a beneficial side effect to the critic's death. We had exhausted the chain of clues at the theater. Milton's death re opened the case. There would be phone records and e-mails to trace. Milton met with many people in a day. Someone might have known something, or said something.

Milton wasn't popular among the actors and crew, but all felt the death penalty was too much even for a bad critic. I told Dean that I would have placed Milton in the modern drama and relevant camp led by Eldon until he wrote the glowing review after seeing Midsummer. He might have been a traitor to the cause, or he might have just put one and one together and realized he knew more than he thought. Rufus had figured that out. Milton could have come to the same realization.

Officially, Emma and Maurice's deaths were still regarded as accidents. Was it possible Milton didn't know what he was dealing with? Perhaps he thought he was dealing with prank letters and an amateur pipe bomb in the toilet bombing.

My mother and aunt's visit caused a stir. Fred and the dwarfs said they would have a little reception for them after the play. It would be late for the ladies, but I had rooms for them at a nearby hotel. The Thursday night performance went very well and they enjoyed it. I was puzzled at the stir, but I discovered no one seemed to think I had a mother. The reception turned out to be festive and fun. Aunt Becky had been an English teacher and their friends understood the play and loved the performance.

Skyler came, as did many of the actors. John was a great hit as a TV anchor. He was the morning man, but that was the time they watched most often. All the actors were on their best behavior and mom, my Aunts and their friends were being as bad as they could manage and all was well.

There were photographs of the play and the actors on the walls. Several were of me and one was of me naked as I was taking off my costume. Miss Wilkerson, Aunt Ellen's girlhood friend and noted spinster, saw it and remarked, "My lord Ellen, big things do come in small packages." She moved on to the next photo without batting an eye.

They went to the hotel, happy and slightly tipsy. I had breakfast with them in the hotel's palm court the next morning. I had been classified as a problem child, although my Aunts and Mom never agreed with that description. They felt vindicated. It was a good and enjoyable experience for all of them.

Hank appeared at three Friday afternoon. He had gotten wind of Milton's death and he was worried. "My son hated that man's guts. He almost killed my daughter-in-law."

"She was Ophelia?"

Hank nodded. "She dated Henry before she met up with Eldon. Henry thinks Eldon likes trophy girlfriends, a harem if possible. He was one of those men who wanted to get the actors into the character and become the character. That meant becoming suicidal for Sue who was playing Ophelia. When Hammerly panned the play Eldon turned on Sue. It was nip and tuck for a while there."

"Henry stayed with her?"

"He did. I told him she wasn't worth it. I was wrong about that. She has been a great mother," Hank said. "Infatuations can do strange things." He paused. "Was I out of line last week when I came over here?"

"No. Why do you think that?"

"You did all the work, I just watched."

"Let me assure you that was not a problem."

"I seem to think about it a lot," Hank said. "I met this other guy who turned me on too."

"Dean?"

"How in hell did you know that?"

"Just a guess. I was guessing you're his type."

"I figured he'd kill me if I made a move," Hank said. "I never guessed. You've..."

"We've had a little fun together," I said. "I have a suspicion you and Dean would have a lot of fun." We talked for a while. Hank was semi-retired and his wife was sick, really sick. He was here because Henry was her only child and she was more worried about him, than about herself. Hank was here to calm her down. She was terrified for her son. Hank didn't say it, but I clearly understood his wife wasn't going to make it much longer.

Hank needed a teacher and a guide into the world of man sex. I was overqualified for the task. Hank helped for the Friday night performance, but Hank came over to my apartment in the morning. Sue needed some time without her father-in-law in the house.

He knocked at my apartment door. I just happened to have Steve, the photographer, with me. I gave Hank a cup of coffee and we got naked. Steve and Hank hit it off. We made a little daisy chain on my bed. I sucked Hank as he sucked Steve. Steve completed the chain by sucking me. Steve's cock was easier to take than mine was and Hank liked it. When we switched, it was Hank's time to take my cock. He did that and had no problem.

As soon as I started to suck Hank he started to leak precum. When we switched, Steve's cock was drooling ball juices. It was nice to know we were all revved up. I don't have the easiest cock in the world to suck, but Hank was sure giving it the good old college try. He wasn't just pretending to be interested either.

Someone knocked on the door. I put on a robe and answered it. Dean was standing there. I told him I was having some fun and he was free to join us. He pretended to be unwilling but he started to take off his shirt as we talked. He wasn't that shy or sincere. When he saw Hank, it looked as if Christmas had come early for both men. Dean got hard the second he saw Hank. All was well.

I was in a rare situation. I was with three men, none of whom were bottoms. That cut my normal repertoire of sexual positions in half. Steve was timid and Hank and Dean were new to the scene. I love my cock, but it ain't for novices.

# Part 9

I thought my foursome was going to be a quiet and restrained event. I soon realized I was in a testosterone storm. Steve, Hank and Dean were conventional men in conventional jobs. They had none of the trappings and baggage the media demands of gay men. When we got together at my apartment all the usual things that restrain their sexual inhibitions were gone. The three men were mutually attracted, but Hank, who was new to the gay scene, really found Steve and Dean attractive.

My previous meetings with them had been more to satisfy their curiosity than their desire to have sex. I had been fucked, but they were too cautious to take the dive with me. This morning they seemed to have made peace with their taste for man sex and were willing to do some experimenting.

Steve had bottomed before, but the other men were new to it. Hank was totally new to it, but he liked Steve and was greatly attracted to

Dean. For a woman getting fucked is like playing with a loaded gun. She doesn't know when it's going to shoot. Even when she's careful there a chance one of the little pollywogs will find a home.

The repercussions for men are much reduced, but the loaded gun aspect remains. Somehow I got the impression Hank would have liked to give Dean's prostate a sperm bath, and wouldn't have minded having his prostate get a buff and shine by Dean's knob. It turned out I was right about that.

Steve had built up his nerve and had a change of heart. He decided to let me stretch his hole and get deep into his ass. As sometimes happens as you think about my cock you get an itch only it can scratch. If you think you might want to try it, you might as well do it. You don't run into cocks as big as mine often.

Fucking never strikes me as a pretty thing to watch. In general, sex is a participatory sport, not a spectator activity. When you watch guys sucking you can see the way a man slicks the knob, and how he takes the cock. Because you need to breathe, you get to see a lot of the cock. Fucking is different. Once you're in you're in. The cock works its magic out of view. It's better if the cock is long and you can see the shaft on the outstroke, but it's mostly out of sight.

Dean and Hank watched as I screwed Steve. They seemed to find it both educational and exciting. Steve was a good sport and had exhibitionist tenancies. He liked the bottom, but he really liked have two men watching him as I worked my meat into his hole. It took a while and Hank and Dean liked the show. I was at the uppermost range of cocks Steve could take and there were some bumps in the road.

It turned into a group fuck. Dean and Hank wanted to see me get deep, so they were part cheerleaders and part coaches. Dean held Steve's legs open while Hank kept the lubricant and the poppers ready. They encouraged Steve and were ready with lubricant to ease my cock into the hole. Our quartet played well together. Dean spurted a few volleys of his seed into the air when I skewered Steve. The other men appreciated that.

I was concentrating on Steve, but I noticed Hank was spending more time with his lubricant coated fingers in Steve's ass. He liked it. Hank also caught a whiff of the poppers. That I discovered was the key to his interest in man sex.

As I fucked, I knew the juices would be bubbling in the other men's balls. I pulled out a few times and Hank took my place in Steve's ass. I could see Steve's excitement grow as his ass lips welcomed Hank's meat. It was good for both of them. Hank pulled out when he got too close. When I re-entered Steve's ass, I sensed he was more relaxed and receptive. I was going to give Dean some quality time in Steve's rectum, but I shot off before I had a chance to trade places with him.

Dean was the only one not to have popped. Hank had become a lot more open-minded once he got into the swing of things. He got on the bed and hoisted up his legs. He was more than willing for Dean to get his rocks off in his body. I have friends who like to pop virgins, but that's not my thing. Hank had never been fucked and Dean had never fucked a man before, so they were equally inexperienced. I soon realized natural sexual drive and a few snorts of Jungle Juice were all they needed.

When I take poppers my sex drive skyrockets. For some reason, I also seem to get an itch deep in my ass that only an oozing cock can scratch. Poppers had exactly the same effect on Hank. He was also a no pain, no gain man. Dean was well hung and it wasn't easy to get it in the first time, but Hank was game.

If hot, sweaty sex between middle-aged men is your thing, Dean and Hank were as good as it gets. Plain old-fashioned lust can do a lot when the problem is a tight ass. We played for about an hour. I wasn't the center of attention. I had been the spark plug, but once

Dean, Hank and Steve got the hang of it, they went at it like dogs in heat.

While the sex was good for me, the investigation didn't seem to be getting anywhere. Dean was checking the people late critic, Milton Hammerly, had talked to in his last days. That turned out to be a huge job. He had talked with 30 to 40 people on the last day of his life. The critic was a social butterfly and he must have run into a hundred people in his last week of life. A good percentage of these were associated with the theater.

Some people think hard work is at the core of detective work, and I agree with that. I have to add that good luck can play a role. There was an anti-gay aspect to the case. I have always assumed that being anti-gay and a closet case were synonyms. I was the bait needed to catch a deeply closeted suspect.

You can't trick Mother Nature and closet cases can't avoid being attracted to cock. Like most men, gay or straight, a big cock has some allure. I'm attractively hung, but that only counts when I'm naked. Dressed I'm a short, ugly hairball. Advertising my cock in public would get me arrested.

In my role as the Wall in Midsummer Night's Dream, I was extensively photographed. Most of these were publicity shots that got wide distribution. Skyler was a costume designer on the make and he made sure the photos got everywhere. My costume was imaginative and unusual as well as successful. I also had done some poses in the photography studio that turned out well. Henry had taken some candid shots of me getting dressed and undressed.

In some of the publicity photos, you could tell I was either well hung, or well padded. In the candid photos, there was no question. I hadn't known the photos were being taken, so they were truly candid. They weren't sexual other than me being naked.

Those nude photos weren't widely distributed, but they were seen by people in the theater and photography community. Liz and Steve were submitting some of them for an award in a photography show so they were on display, but not published in the newspaper.

I was leaving the theater after a high school matinée and Gustav, the former Chairman of the theater department came up to me. "You have made quite a splash in the theater world," he said. "I'm teaching at Central High School and I have a hard time making them understand that every role counts, even the minor ones," he said.

"Well you can't be much more minor than playing a wall," I said.

"You were perfect. Skyler has never been this inventive before," Gustav continued. "The stars were in alignment. Do you have time to have a drink? My apartment is a few blocks away."

I said sure. There was no evening performance so I was free. Gustav lived in a renovated loft apartment in what had been a bank. It was nicely furnished in a post-divorce style with inexpensive Ikea type furniture and theatrical props. It was nice, but not fancy,

Gustav was a drinker of the old style. He had bourbon, Scotch and Gin. He was a martini man; I went for bourbon. He also had cheese and crackers. He wasn't a Velveeta or American cheese man. I seem to have been losing my redneck tastes. The cheese was good, but wasn't the usual arty type. I asked him about them. He was from Wisconsin, and these were locally made there in small creameries. As we talked I had several rather stiff drinks and was getting happy.

On the table he had a portfolio of photos. He showed it to me. It was a collection of photographic prints of me getting into the wall costume. These were less arty and more naked than the ones on display. These photos featured my cock much more prominently. I wasn't hard or anything like that, but they were definitely photos of my cock. Some were high focus photos close-ups showing my meat in detail.

"I haven't seen these photos before," I said. "The photography class has been holding out on me."

"They weren't suitable for the general public," Gustav explained. "I saw them and they gave me a few I admired. They're fine photos. It's a pity the public isn't more tolerant of male nudity. I had one blown up." He went to his bedroom and brought back a poster sized print. It was a detail of my cock. It looked like one of those high-resolution photographs of hilly terrain. It took a few seconds of looking before you realized what it was. It was of my cock head sheathed in the foreskin. Every nook and cranny was sharp and detailed. At the center was the pucker of skin at the tip covering my cock head. The gap in the pucker looked like the entrance to a cave.

"Damn, I've never seen it blown up like that," I said. I couldn't think of anything else to say. "It looks like you could mountain climb on it."

"It's a beautiful photograph," Gustav said.

"Is it the photograph or the subject matter?"

"At first I thought it was the photo," he replied. He looked me in the eye. "I assume you know that's not true. Self-delusion is a universal human characteristic. It took some doing to admit to myself I was as turned on as I was. I hope I'm not offending or shocking you."

I smiled. "It takes quite a bit to offend or shock me. I've come to the conclusion interest in other men's cocks is pretty close to being a universal male characteristic. Believe me, you aren't the first."

Gustav looked embarrassed. After a pause he asked, "I would love to see it. For real. Would you do that?"

"I'm not much of a show and tell guy," I said. Poor Gustav looked disappointed. "I don't mind some playtime. Could you do that?" I think I had more bourbon than I realized.

Gustav nodded.

"Well let's get naked and go to it," I said. He led me to his bedroom. The bedroom and bath were the only enclosed rooms in the loft apartment. They were more poster-sized photos of my cock there. "You are really into my cock, aren't you?" I asked as I took my shirt off. He nodded. As I dropped my pants, Gustav dropped to his knees.

Now, I'm not exactly a virgin and it took me no more than five or ten seconds to know Gustav wasn't as inexperienced as he said he was. When I saw all the photographic blow-ups I was afraid he might have a problem. He seemed obsessed as he swallowed my cock I knew there was no problem. He was a lover and a cocksucker. He worshiped my cock. It was more like a sexual-religious experience than basic man lust.

The bigger I got the better Gustav liked it. He began to moan when my precum began to flow. He continued to worship my cock. I asked him if he wanted the thicker stuff.

"The cream?"

"Do you want it?"

"Oh yes!" he said.

"Do you want me to tell you when I'm going to shoot, or just let it rip?"

"Surprise me!" Gustav cried. A few seconds later he had a mouthful of my Red-Neck High Test. He didn't stop sucking when I stopped shooting. He kept on sucking until I was drained.

"Do you like getting fucked by any chance?" I asked.

"I do, but I'm not in your league," Gustav said. He looked at me. "Could I suck your cock again?"

I smiled. He returned to my crotch. We sixty-nined. His cock was mostly a big mushroom on a Popsicle stick. His juices were flowing like Niagara Falls. If anything he was better the second time. I don't mind being worshiped once and a while even if it is only my cock. I asked if he wanted me to take his load. He told me not to worry; he was hard to get off. After he took my second load, we talked.

"Somehow I had the impression you were anti-gay?" I asked.

"I suspect you've guessed I was one of those who doth protest too much," Gustav said. "I sometime amaze myself at my abilities in self-delusion. For fifty-five years, I lived in fear someone would discover my dreadful secret. I was terrified and hoped if I was anti-gay enough I'd turn straight."

"Did it work?"

"My wife left me. She said I had turned mean," Gustav said. "It took me a year or two to realize she was right and to figure out why I had turned nasty. You know about the poison pen letters?"

"Yes."

"I wasn't directly involved, but in retrospect I was stirring the pot. I think I was playing with fire and didn't know what would happen. I was away for the last two weeks in Chicago judging an awards program. I didn't know of the deaths in Midsummer."

"Do you know who was in the pot you were stirring?"

"Eldon was involved."

"He's anti-gay?"

"I don't think so. He does nothing unless there is something in it for him. Back then, I thought he was my friend and was trying to help me out. He was actually trying to get my job and helping me crash and burn. He should have been a great actor. He can play two roles at the same time. He's a piece of work," Gustav said.

"Was he involved in the letters?"

"I have always doubted he would actually do anything himself," he said. "He's too smart for that. He's a very bitter man. His schemes have all come to naught. Some day he might blow up. As far as I can tell, he's not at that point yet."

"How about his harem?"

"I don't know whose left. Eldon tends to wear out friends. They don't last if they're lucky. They find out the truth." He was silent for a few moments. "For your information Eldon may be straight, but he fucked me two years ago. It wasn't a good experience. He's hung, not like you, but he's hung."

"Poor technique?"

"I wasn't a voluntary participant. He's a role player. I was the fag he had to fuck to teach me a lesson. It was the Drill Sergeant and the enlistee type stuff," he explained. "I wasn't playing the same game. If you ever feel the desire to tear a guy a new ass hole, let me recommend Eldon."

I had to get home, so I let Gustav suck me off one more time and I left.

The next day was the last performance and a full house. It was a celebratory evening. Most of the cast and crew went to a bar for a party. I went to the party for a while, but was tired and left early. That turned out to be a mistake. What exactly happened I don't know. I woke up a day later in the hospital with John, my contractor friend, and my mother by my side. I had one hell of a headache. I had been unconscious with a serious concussion after someone attacked me from the rear. The doctor's told me I was one short step from having a skull fracture.

I got out of the hospital two days later, but I was out of commission for two weeks. Dean came by to get my story. I wasn't helpful since I was just a victim and saw nothing. He had some interesting information. I wasn't robbed, but there had been an attempted rape. It was attempted only because the rapist had a problem with premature ejaculation.

"Did you get a sample?" I asked.

"We sure as shit did," Dean replied. We both knew in this post DNA age sperm is the ultimate clue. Dean also had samples from recent rapes and they were undergoing analysis and comparison. Two days later Dean called; he had a match.

The man who assaulted me had also assaulted Sue, Henry's wife and the ill-fated Ophelia. This was news to me. Apparently, the suicide attempt followed a sexual assault. Sue took an over dose and was found unconscious. Dean said she denied knowing anything about the assault.

"Could the assault have occurred after the overdose?" I asked.

"Damn, we may have missed something big here," Dean said. He called the detective in charge, a woman named Rosa Montague. We he was done with the conversation he told me what he had found out.

"Rosa's a good woman. The victim was in shock and very fragile. She insisted she hadn't tried to kill herself and she hadn't been assaulted. She was very confused and Rosa thought maybe it was a love affair gone bad. The boyfriend was there and Rosa figured the girl didn't want him to know. Rosa did get a DNA sample from the boyfriend and it definitely wasn't him."

"Henry's a good man," I added.

"There was one aspect of the assault you might find interesting." Dean paused.

"Spill it out," I said. "I've still got a headache and I don't need suspense."

"The victim wasn't penetrated; it was a case of premature ejaculation."

"I take it the case is being reopened?" I asked.

"Rosa doing a search of all cases that involving premature ejaculation as we speak," Dean added. "We've been investigating the wrong fucking case. I had it pegged as an artsy-fartsy case of professional jealousy. It's sex crime, a pervert getting his rocks off."

"Shakespeare would never let that happen. Sex, power and money are the key for him," I said. "Where did Eldon work before he came here? I might check and see if there are similar cases there." Dean left like a bloodhound that suddenly discovered the scent of his prey.

# Part 10

My career as a Shakespearean Wall was over and I returned to my normal work. Dean was hot on the trail of my assailant and the murderer of three people. You would have thought there would be a public outcry about so many killings, but our victims were short on the requirements for public outcries. Not one of them was a young, blond woman. Our only woman victim, Emma, had mousy brown hair and was in her later thirties. No one cared about Emma.

The attack on me had been good luck in one respect. Rapists with a problem with premature ejaculation were a special breed, and somewhat rare. It also eliminated all women from our suspect list. Computers are wonderful things, and they turned up an additional similar case in Richmond, two in Madison, Wisconsin and several in Ann Arbor, Michigan. Dean was trying to connect our Richmond suspects with the mid-western crimes. He noted both Madison and Ann Arbor were college towns.

While the investigation proceeded, Freddy gave me a call. He was back in New York and there was going to be a festival of young theater companies in an Off Broadway theater. A foundation was sponsoring four companies to do a week of performances as part of a summer festival. They had just selected the Duke of Richmond's Company. The good review in the Washington Post had done the trick.

This was a dream come true for the actors and production staff. It was both recognition and a chance to hit the big time. The other companies were from Boston, San Francisco and St. Louis, much bigger cities than Richmond. Freddy wanted me to be there. "You know Skyler's design for your costume was a masterpiece. It requires your semi naked body to make it work," Freddy explained. "I know you aren't planning a career in the theater, but you could help make this thing work."

I wasn't sure I wanted to take two weeks off. "Think of it as a vacation. Have you been to New York?" he asked.

"Never for more than a day and mostly passing through," I admitted. "It's hard to get a grip on it."

"I'm a native and will guarantee you will love the place after I've shown you around," Freddy said with great enthusiasm. "To tell you the truth, I would like to have you here to keep an eye on things. They haven't captured the murderer yet. If jealousy is part of the motive, then this trip to Broadway is like adding salt an open wound." I said I'd think about it.

The next day Charlie Smith, the director, officially made the official request to I continue in the role. Fifteen minutes later Skyler called. He was damn close to begging me to go with them to New York. "Let me be frank," he said, "I've tried the costume on several other guys. It simply doesn't work. I need you."

"Shit, I'm just playing a wall!"

"You are a perfect wall," Skyler exclaimed. "The stars are in alignment for this production. Most of the people involved are talented and gifted, but that doesn't mean shit in the theater. Sometimes things just don't click, or the right people don't see the play, or they see it on a bad night. This could have been a good production, but it turned into magic. The closest I've been to Broadway is suburban Philadelphia. 99.9 percent of the theater people only get to buy tickets on Broadway. This is our chance."

I decided to play the wall in New York. The next several months were frantic in Richmond. Most of the actors needed to cover their day jobs, or to arrange for vacation time. The foundation sponsoring the festival paid for most of the production, but travel, rooms, food and other expenses were born by the Duke of Richmond's Company. Fund raising was going on behind the scenes. I called Dean and told him about the production in New York. He was hard at work on the rape connection, checking on men who had been to Madison and Ann Arbor.

He also said he would contact the NYPD and warn them about the situation. He agreed with Freddy. The visit to Broadway might inspire the murderer. Two weeks later, I went on a weekend trip to New York for advance publicity. I went with Charlie, Skyler and John Smithers, our weatherman. Freddy and the dwarfs were in New York already.

We went up in a van with some of the costumes. There was to be a photo shoot and several interviews. The whole thing was rushed, but Skyler told me one of the four companies originally selected to give performances pulled out at the last moment and we were substitutes. A young man named Russell met us at the Foundation's headquarters on East 87th street. The top floor had an apartment for guests. We got the van parked. That was an adventure. Russell couldn't have been more than 25 or 27 years old, but he was helpful and eager to please.

The photo shoot was going to be early the next day in Greenwich Village. We would need to get to the studio at 7:00 to be ready by 8:30. Skyler thought that was too early. Russell explained the photographer had done a complete spread on the company that had withdrawn, so it was hard to work it into his schedule. We went out to dinner in a small restaurant nearby. The food was good.

We got back to the apartment by 10:00. Russell lived on Long Island so getting home and then back to the city by 6:00 in the morning wasn't an easy task. John suggested that he spend the night with us. Russell looked a bit like John's lover Lance, and I think he may have had plans. John and Charlie shared the master bedroom that had its own bath. Skyler and I took the other and we had a bath down the hall. Russell was on the couch.

I fell asleep right off the bat. When I woke at 5:30, Russell was in bed with Skyler. I didn't know Skyler was that fast. Russell was sitting on Skyler's cock moaning softly. I went over to then and fed Russell my cock. That seemed to push him over the edge. He shot off. Skyler got up, rolled him over and made an early morning deposit in Russell's ass. We all showered, got in the van and made it to the studio by 7:00. I knew New York was big, but I was surprised how far away the Village was. I sort of visualized Central Park, Rockefeller Center and Greenwich Village being within blocks of each other.

Freddy, Rudy and David were waiting for us. The photographer was grumpy, but warmed up considerably when we got in costume. Actually, he warmed up when he saw me naked as I got dressed. Two more photographers, Sal and Ira, arrived for the shoot. Don, the foundation's photographer, called them. We were there for three hours.

Don asked if I could stay for additional hour or so. He said he would get me back to the foundation's headquarters by 4:00, when we had interviews scheduled. That was fine with me, but I told him they needed to check with Skyler. My costume was difficult to take off. It was okay with him so the rest left me with Don and his friends. I heard Don say, "Believe me taking the costume off won't be a problem at all." Skyler laughed.

Don, Sal and Ira were good photographers and nice guys, but I soon noticed their interest in me wasn't 100% platonic. My interest in them wasn't that platonic either. They were all my type. Sal was a beefy, hairy Italian. Ira was a fireplug of a man. Don was tall and imposing. He wore boxers and was imposing that way too.

I wasn't sure how they would make the transition from a publicity photo shoot to sex, but I suspected at least one of the trio of photographers had some thoughts on the subject. The photographer and his model is the basis of 50% of the porn movies made, so I figured something would happen.

During a break, Don came over to me and whispered, "Sal's a little embarrassed, but he wants to know if size queens bother you?"

"Not particularly," I answered. "They seem to come with the territory." I looked him in the eye. "Is he the only size queen here?"

Don smiled. "In round numbers you could estimate there are about three in the studio. Two of us are lookers. Sal would like more."

"I'm a top."

"Skyler told Sal that," Dan said, "and that's what excites him. Do you have a problem with pictures?"

"I do. I'm a private investigator and go undercover. I don't like my face to be seen."

Don laughed. "It's not your face I'm interested in. Sal likes anatomical photos. You know, close ups and detailed views."

Against my better judgment, I agreed. I wasn't sure I would get hard with a camera present, but that wasn't a problem at all. Sal stripped and naked he was my kind of man. At 5'-8", he was a muscle man, firm and solid. Curly black hair covered him from his neck to his toes. Uncut, he possessed double the skin he needed to sheath his cock. He helped me get out of my costume and then went for my cock. We sucked and then sixty-nined. Sal wanted more.

He looked as if he had buns of steel, but where there is a will, there is a way. Sal wanted my cock bad and was willing put up with some pain. I'm not into pain, so I used half a tube of lube and took my time. Don took pictures and provided the lube. Ira gave advice. He had quite a store of knowledge on how to get an oversized cock into a tight ass. Sal finally surrendered and my cock slid deep into his ass. Sal shivered as I went deep. I liked that reaction. I hate it when you do all that work and your partner doesn't like it that much.

I took my time and discovered Sal liked deep, long strokes. I pulled out all the way several times to lubricate my cock. Each time I did this he was more open and took my cock more easily. His reaction was better too. Eventually, he zoned out and just went with the flow. His only job was to moan, twitch and quiver.

Don wasn't straight with me in one respect. He and Ira weren't just lookers. When Sal finally shot off, I pulled out and rested. I went to the toilet room to clean up. Ira joined me. He was naked by now.

"I've never been with an uncut man before," Ira almost whispered. He was shivering a little. I think it was both very uneasy and very excited. "Does it get kind of messy in there?"

"In the days before regular showers I guess it could be a bit gamy," I replied. "Some guys like it that way. I have disappointed a few customers who were hoping for something really ripe."

Ira watched me clean my cock. I skinned it back and cleaned my head and then the skin. I assumed Ira was Jewish and was uneasy.

"I've never seen a cock as totally... Gentile as yours," he said.

I smiled. "You can't decide it that's good or bad, can you?"

Ira smiled. "It would be a lot easier to make a decision if I wasn't so turned on."

"I'm not sure my cock has a religion, or if it does it's a really ancient one," I said. Ira finally let his cock do the thinking. He dropped to his knees and sucked me. He got my skin-covered head into his mouth, and looked up. At first, I thought he was looked at me, but I think he was doing a quick check for lightning bolts. Lightning didn't strike and he relaxed.

Don and Sal came in the room and joined us. This time Sal took the photos. Don was naked now. He was mostly smooth, but well-built and nicely hung. I sucked Don as Ira sucked me. Don had one of those cocks that drooped when he was hard. It was perfect for deep throating. Ira shifted his location and I felt his cock at my ass. I moved a little to give him better access.

Ira's cock was mostly a big, flared head on a thin shaft and it felt great. It rubbed my prostate just the right way. We switched around a few times and eventually Ira got a mouthful of gentile man seed served directly from a foreskin-covered cock. We all had a good time. I had to get back to the foundation for the interviews, so I got dressed. They were all good about schedules. Don said they'd be sure to get to the performance.

The interviews were good. One critic went after Charlie for using the dwarfs in a freak show. Rudy and David took care of that in brisk fashion. They made it clear they were fully capable of selecting the shows they wanted to perform in and they didn't need a patronizing "protector" to look after their welfare.

John discussed the advantages of clearly differentiation the three groups of characters. The elegant courtiers, the rude mechanicals and the fairies were all clearly defined and made the complicated play much more easily understood. "I'm quite sure Shakespeare would have used Dwarfs, giants and cute dogs if it served his dramatic purpose," he added.

The next day was available for site seeing. It was a rainy day. The Foundation headquarters was a few blocks from the Metropolitan Museum so Freddy and Rudy took me there. I loved it. There's a big difference between reading or hearing about something and seeing it in person. The Egyptian stuff was great, much nicer than in the Three Stooges meet the Mummy type movies. I like the Roman and Greek statues too. I had a great time.

That evening, I got a call from Dean. "Eldon directed a play in Ann Arbor at the time of one of the rapes. He was teaching at a school in southern Wisconsin at the time. Ann Arbor and Madison were an easy drive for him," he said.

"It's time for a DNA sample," I said.

"Not as easy as you would think," Dean replied. "He seems to be on sabbatical."

"How in hell did he manage that? He's not in an academic job anymore?"

"It seems to be a homemade sabbatical. He told his employer he was going to take a year off and work on writing a play," Dean explained. "He left without pay and without a forwarding address. He's vanished. His ex-wife is mad as shit. Without pay seems to have translated into without child support."

"Has anyone else vanished?"

"The illusive Mr. Fenton has disappeared too. When we questioned him two months ago, he wasn't helpful. He had been an undergraduate at the school Tony taught at," Dean said. "We went to talk with him last week and he was gone. The landlord said he went back to his poor widowed mother in Iowa. The widow turned out to be a widower, and he wasn't on talking terms with his son. I got the impression Fenton had left home with a cloud over his head."

"What was the nature of the cloud?"

"The Father wouldn't say. I called the local police Chief," Dean continued. "Fenton was a bit rough with one of the local girls. It wasn't particularly clear-cut, but his getting out of town wasn't voluntary. He had a partner in crime who left town with him. He ended up in Richmond too. That is Robert Miller, the guy who played Thisbe in the play."

"Holy shit!" I exclaimed. "He was pretty much an asshole throughout the production. Where is he?"

"He's left town too, with no forwarding address," Dean said. "He could have been just a spy or the perpetrator. The Police chief said he was he school bully." After we finished the call, I gave the information to Charlie. He knew Robert had left Richmond and had to recast the part. He knew nothing of the connection to Eldon.

Robert was at very least a spy and possibly more than a spy. He struck me as a whiner not a doer. It was possible Maurice caught him doing something. I didn't know if Maurice would have confronted him, or reported back to Skyler. Perhaps Robert thought Maurice had seen something.

I went to dinner at Freddy's apartment with the rest of the group. Robert's relationship to Fenton and Eldon was a shock to everyone. It did explain how the poison pen letter writer knew so much about the actors. No one knew much about Robert.

"He was a pretty common type of person you find coming to auditions," Charlie said. "He was born to be a spear carrier, but had dreams of stardom."

"I thought he suffered the most common problems of his type. He thought he should be a star and the roles he had were beneath him," Freddy remarked. "He wasn't a particularly good spear carrier. Some actors have the ability to make an impression in a minor role. Robert wasn't willing to do that. He wasn't bad enough to lose the part, but not good enough to shine. I got my start doing a first rate gravedigger in Hamlet. I've never played the Danish Prince, but I made all the way up to Polonius a few times."

"Do you think Eldon, Fenton and Robert left because of the New York run?" Skyler asked.

"Maybe, but is more likely the Richmond Police were on their trail and they knew it," I said. "Eldon and Fenton knew the police had suspicions. It would be a good time to leave town."

"The pettiness of the poison pen letters was a red herring," I said. "We have three deaths and multiple rapes. We are dealing with your basic homicidal manic sex pervert."

"It seems odd to me the rapist didn't kill his victims and the murderer didn't rape his victims," Frederic observed. "I think a murder-rapist is the more usual combination. Could we have two disturbed minds? Perhaps they share a common grudge, but they have independent modus operandi? Or is that modi operandi? My Latin is rusty."

"Modi operandi has a ring to it," Skyler said. "Since Robert was most probably the spy, prankster and letter writer, I will bet Maurice discovered something."

"Would Maurice report back to you or confront the man if he discovered something?" I asked.

"Maurice was a flaming faggot, but he was no coward, and no shrinking violet," Skyler explained. "I had a friend who referred to him as an attack Chihuahua."

"I wonder if Maurice found out, confronted him, and then Robert killed him?" I said, thinking out loud. "Perhaps Robert found out he liked killing. The pace of deaths is remarkable."

"The earlier outbreak of poison pen letters never moved beyond the prank level," Charlie said. "I get the impression things were spiraling out of control. I can see why Emma died. She could spill the beans and her efforts at bombing were so amateurish, she was sure to be caught, but Milton's death was gratuitous."

"Has Robert discovered a taste for murder?" Frederic asked.

Eldon, Robert, Eileen and Fenton were perfectly good suspects, and almost certainly were involved. It was hard to allocate the individual crimes to particular suspects. I had tentatively assigned the poison pen letters to Robert, the rapes to Fenton and the murder to Eldon. Eileen could have done the letters and murders, but could not have been the rapist.

We returned to Richmond the next day. The play would open in two months. I got involved in another case and didn't devote much time to the murders. The City Police were taking care of that.

My new case was a particularly nasty accusation of child molestation in an upscale private school, the Dominion Academy. It was the sort of story that could have destroyed the school and the lives of several teachers. The headmaster of the school was pompous and pretentious, but one of the board members called me and said she suspected something wasn't kosher.

Part of the problem was the Headmaster. He didn't know his staff well enough to trust them, so when the accusation was made, he was clueless. The family involved was new to Richmond. They were threatening to go public if the school didn't pay up. They seemed to feel $500,000.00 would solve the problem. The alleged victim and her mother burst into hysterics at the drop of a hat, and it was hard to get a clear story. The alleged perpetrator was a fifty-three

year old female science teacher, Betty Wood. She was of the type
my aunts would describe as hard but fair. She was married but a bit
mannish in her mannerisms. This was one of those situations where
the accusation could be as bad as an actual conviction. Reputations
would be ruined either way.

The woman's students were shocked and incredulous at the
accusations. That included several who didn't like Mrs. Wood. They
may not have liked her, but they didn't think she did, or could have
done anything improper.

The family of the victim was hard to trace. The mother remarried
twice, so the family name changed. We finally figured it out. This
was the third time the family made similar accusations. Once was in
a nursery school and once in a grade school. In each case the schools
had paid. We found out the fathers in the previous cases got 10% of
the take and a roll in the hay with the mother. The marriages lasted a
year and a half and the divorce proceedings were in the works as soon
as the schools made the settlement.

We also talked to the doctor who examined the girl after the
molestation. The mother told the school he had found clear evidence
of the event. The headmaster had been so concerned with keeping it
quiet, he hadn't confirmed it with the doctor. Much to my surprise,
the girl had been molested. The doctor had sperm samples to prove
it. I was never that good at science, but sperm samples pretty much
left Mrs. Woods in the clear.

I called the police on this and they discovered the mother had been
giving her current hubby free samples of her daughter. Apparently, it
wasn't exactly rape; it was very illegal.

The school had an earlier problem with a faculty member. Eldon Jones
taught there for two years after leaving Byrd University. Fortunately,
Dominion's Art Teacher, Donnie Donne, noticed Eldon was getting
too close to several students. Donnie was talented, energetic and

gay as a goose. He was into older men and was careful to insure he avoided any inappropriate contact with students. Several members of the board were gunning for him because he obviously was gay and he wouldn't give them any reason to attack him.

I interviewed him for the current case and accidentally discovered the connection with Eldon. "Mr. Jones was planning to take some students on a retreat. It was to "eat, drink and breath theater event" he said. Students and faculty don't go anywhere without school approval. If he was talking them on a day trip Shakespeare Theater in Washington the school might approve. This was going to be a weekend visit to a cottage in West Virginia owned by a friend of his." Donnie said.

"Overnight trips require a faculty member or two and a parent at a minimum. Eldon was an impressive man in some ways, especially if you are immature. He liked to have admirers nearby, doting on every pearl of wisdom. He believed if you are talented enough you don't need training," Donnie continued. "I think that is a crock of shit, but it is exactly was young students want to hear. It's the quick and easy fantasy of instant fame."

"Do you know where the cottage was?" I asked.

"No, I didn't get any of the details," he replied. "He didn't own it. It belonged to a friend."

"Did you get the name of the friend?"

"Let me think. Ellie? Ellen? It was something like that," Donnie said. "I remember thinking Eldon and Ellie sounded like a purveyor of gourmet jellies. Ellie isn't quite right."

"Emma perhaps? How about Eileen?"

"Eileen, that's it! I think I met her once, she was doing a scene from Shakespeare for the class once," Donnie replied. "She was one of those people who are rude out of principle." As soon as I finished with Donnie I called Dean and told him to check out Eileen's land holdings.

A day later, Dean came by and gave me an update. Eileen had burned many bridges in her life and her father and stepmother weren't helpful. Her father simply wouldn't talk about her. The stepmother was willing to complain bitterly about Eileen.

When asked if Eileen had a cabin or cottage, the stepmother said no. In the background Dean heard the father say, "What about Uncle Tom's Cabin?" after much discussion it appeared Eileen's uncle left her a cabin near the Virginia border in the Appalachians. They didn't know exactly where it was, but knew the name of the county. Fortunately, the Uncle was named Thomas Wynnbourn Faversham. With our luck he would have been named John Smith.

The name was easy to trace and they found the property. The West Virginia State Police went to investigate. The house was empty but Eldon, Eileen and Fenton's cars were there. It had been empty for at least several days.

On a hunch, Dean asked if Uncle Tom had a car. He did and the license had recently been renewed. Uncle Tom had died eight years earlier, but West Virginia didn't have computerized cross checking between license and death notices. He had owned an old Bronco, so the car was big enough to hold them all with their luggage. Our suspects were on the move.

Charlie started refresher rehearsals the next day. The trip to New York was two weeks away. Robert was gone and a cheerful kid named Maury took his place. Maury was a natural comedian and he took the role seriously. As Thisbe, he was a natural. Maury was almost as hairy as me, so Skyler redesigned the costume to be skimpier. Maury could do a funny falsetto, and did a schoolboy's imitation of feminine mannerisms. The combination was great. My wall, Frederic's Bottom and Maury's Thisbe were all properly outlandish.

When looking through the chink in the wall, that is between my legs, Maury made great show of lifting my balls out of the way to see better. That almost stopped the show it was so funny. Maury was not opposed to copping a feel, but he had an impish quality and it was funny without overly sexual overtones. Most assumed he just was shifting my costume. The costume just barely covered my balls, so it was real.

I had my security people on the watch as the departure date got closer. The city police were on watch too. State Troopers were all looking for Uncle Tom's Bronco, but there was no sign of it yet.

Two days before we left, we put on a full-scale performance. This was treated as a fund-raiser to help finance the trip. There was a $25.00 base ticket price and a required donation. Anything over the $25.00 price was tax deductible. They sold like hotcakes. The governor actually attended.

Hank and his wife returned for the performance. I could see she had declined since the last time I saw her. They were with her sister and brother-in law. He would be going to New York with us to watch after Henry.

The performance went off well, and the minor changes Charlie made with Maury worked very well. There was a post play reception. We rustics remained in costume and did a repeat of the final dance. It was most successful and we taught the First Lady and her daughters the steps. We had a day of rest, followed by the bus trip to Manhattan.

My plan had been to stay with Frederic. Hank decided we would stay together in the same place. This made security easier. Frederic and the Elves were going to join us even though they lived in New York. There were way too many deaths in Richmond to take a risk.

Frederic grumbled about this, but he knew there was danger. He was irreplaceable. He alone could do Bottom with the skill needed. We stayed in a building called the Rehearsal Center. It had been some sort of a YMCA building with several gym sized rooms, some private bedrooms and an open dormitory space. It had served as a homeless shelter before the foundation that sponsored the plays converted it to its current use.

The dormitory was an open room with room for 30 or 40 beds. It was normally used for rehearsals, but the foundation brought in cots and screens to restore the room to its original use. They used some theatrical sets to spiff up the room and they had some tents from a production of Camelot subdividing the space. A clever interior decorator had been at work. We all shared a gang shower, except for the private bedrooms, which had their own baths.

We were given a choice where we wanted to stay. The gay portion of the crew chose the dorm; the straight portion of the crew took the bedrooms. That worked out well. We went to dinner and had a tour of the theater that evening. While it was about the same size as the theater we used in Richmond, the stage was much better equipped and the lighting more elaborate. Stoner and the rest of the lighting crew would have their work cut out for them.

We got back to the rehearsal center. It had a guard and a NYPD cruiser was nearby. It was a hot day and the shower was soon in use. You might think a big, open room filled with gay men with an attached gang shower would be a recipe for an orgy, but you would have been wrong, for the first hour at least. I will admit the dress code became very informal. I was sure portions of the crew had been intimate with other men in the group, but they had never been all naked together.

We sat around wearing a towels or undershorts. The dwarfs skipped the towels all together, and seemed to be the style setters. I had a hard time keeping my towel in place and no one seemed to mind much. A good portion of the group had seen me naked anyway. It turned out nude was better than a wet spot on your shorts. Cocks can't be tricky. When they are excited they show it.

We talked about scheduling for the next few days and planned things out. Charlie was always well organized, but when you were actually there and at the theater, some modifications were needed. Frederic was helpful as always. We went to bed and other than the gentle sucking of cocks and moans during orgasms, all was quiet.

The next day was filled with activity. We unpacked the scenery, worked on the lights and got some actual rehearsing done. The foundation provided some technical staff to help and they got along well with our crew. Theatrical troops are typically filled with oversized egos and attitude. Charlie was anti-attitude and Frederic, who had more experience than the rest of the group combined, was ego free. The group before us was apparently 100% prima donnas, so the New York staff thought they were on vacation with us.

I had a chance to meet with Dean and the NYPD man on the case. God must have created the Bronx so our detective, Saul Horowitz, could be born there. I was surprised the NYPD was that interested, but the city didn't like the idea of out-of-towners being killed on their turf. Saul arrived with the information that Uncle Tom's Bronco was found in a parking lot near a commuter rail station into Manhattan.

"Shit, someone is crazy!" Dean exclaimed. Dean and Saul could hardly be more unalike, but they were in agreement on that. The NYPD would protect the perimeter of the theater, and have undercover men inside. Hank, Randy, who was Charlie's partner and a former Marine, and I were in the dressing rooms and on stage. Photographs of Eldon, Eileen, Fenton and Robert were distributed to the police and to the ushers in the theater.

To say the NYPD was well supplied with bomb sniffing dogs, understates the case. The Bronco had two parking tickets that gave us an approximate time for suspects' arrival in the city. The publicity for the play went into full gear and the photos we had posed for several months earlier were a hit.

As had been the case before with the earlier Richmond production, events conspired to make us more visible. The previous production in the New York festival was poorly received, so the foundation was looking for a hit. The photographs were memorable and distinctive. Skyler's costumes were a marvel, distinctive, unusual and oddly attractive.

We got back to the dormitory at 10:00, exhausted and keyed up. It should be an impossibility to be very tired and very excited at the same time, but that was my situation and most of the other members of the cast felt the same way. The next day would be the dress rehearsal and there was a lot to do and remember.

A long shower would help, but there was a line so I waited until the rush passed. When I got the water going, the shower filled up again. Frederic and the elves joined me, as did Hank. The last to join us was Maury.

We had some nice touch, feel and probe fun, but Rudy pointed to a door on the side of the drying area. It led to a small dance and aerobics studio. It was a windowless interior room with mirrored walls. Charlie and his lover Randy were going at it in one corner.

I have no problem with sex, group sex, or public sex if everyone is into it. I do have a problem keeping men awake who want to sleep. Rudy told me Stoner had found the room the night before and it had become a playroom. As a detective, I was shocked my high-powered detective skills hadn't found the room. I thought I could smell sex from considerable distance. Rudy, David, Samuel and the twins Dan and Don all trooped into the room.

I'm not sure Hank had considered sex with little people before, but Dan and Don took a shine to him. Frederic, Rudy and David played with me and Maury connected with Samuel. In some ways Maury was like me. He had double doses of all the male characteristics but they were assembled without any physical attractiveness. He was all man without being a stud muffin. He wasn't ugly, at least not to me, but I bet he scared kids at the beach. Samuel was smooth and had been uneasy with me when we first met. He was at ease with Maury.

It took a little while for Hank and Maury to get use to the dwarfs as fully sexual people, but they were convincing. Maury took Samuel's cock up his ass, and Hank was fucking Don as Dan plowed his ass. Rudy and David treated Frederic and me as a sexual playground, probing sucking and fucking whoever was nearest.

Skyler, Stoner, our light man, and one of the New York light men came in and they played with Samuel. Maury transferred his interest to me. Dan and Don were much taken with Hank, but Randy, Charlie's lover joined them. He was interested in the twins. I was surprised when Charlie came over to Frederic.

Charlie was a big, almost overweight man, who was always business. I hadn't thought he had a sexual side. Moderately hairy, he had a prematurely middle-aged look. His cock was big and almost overweight too. At first, I thought he might have used a penis pump, but soon realized it was real. It was impressive. He had just fucked his partner, but seemed to want to take a taste of Frederic's cock. That was good and they explored the possibilities. Frederic topped and all was well.

Maury was a surprise. While he felt me out as part of the play, we hadn't connected when not on stage. I soon discovered he was horny as hell and a damn good lover. He seemed to have a snake-like detachable jaw and could deep throat men easily. His ass was elastic and I deep dicked him on my first thrust. Maury had buns of steel, but he open wide on the forward thrust and clenched tightly on the backstroke. It was wonderful.

Everything we did was good. Maury's cock oozed a particularly rich and creamy pre cum. His cock was of average length but had extra girth and was just the right size to serve as a battering ram for my prostate. He was mad with lust when he was ramming my ass, but he would stop just short of an orgasm and pull out.

Charlie had recharged. He was near enough to fill the void left by Maury's withdrawal. I had never been so filled in my life. Charlie was gentle, but even the smallest movements were exciting. The other men had climaxed and they gathered around us and discussed the anatomical improbability that Charlie's cock would fit in my hole. Charlie pulled out and let Maury go at me another time. This time he shot off.

I later fondled Maury's balls and realized his mamma might have been a goat. He gave my rectum a sperm douche. He pulled out and Charlie reentered.

"I've never used cum as a lubricant before," Charlie said. "It's hot. I'm going to shoot soon!"

"Fill him up!" Randy ordered. Charlie's cock all but exploded in my ass. I could feel his sperm ticking my ass.

Things calmed down after that. I showered again and went to bed. No one had any trouble sleeping.

# Part II

Charlie put his organizational skills to the test in the twelve hours before the opening. There seemed to be a million and one things to do, but everyone buckled down and got it done. Skyler was normally a nervous wreck, but was a pillar of strength when necessary.

The theater was empty a half-hour before curtain time. The audience arrived in droves filling every seat. We were busy at the theater. I watched the actors; Hal watched the stage crew. The NYPD was busy outside on the sidewalks. One of the bomb-sniffing dogs struck pay dirt eight blocks away.

Mental illness is a curse but can also be a blessing. I would think that just about everyone in the world would understand New York cops are a bit sensitive on the subject of bombs. They are also constantly looking for them and well equipped to find them. Robert was walking in our direction with another homemade bomb in a suitcase, when Attila, a German shepherd with an unforgiving nature, got a sniff.

I knew from my own experience that to a bomb-sniffing dog, discovering an explosive device was like rolling Christmas, the Fourth of July and your birthday into one glorious event. Attila warned his handler; the cop called in back up. In New York the response time to a bomb is maybe as long as a minute or two. The Police were alert anyway and had preposition a bomb squad van near the theater.

Robert didn't notice at first. Uniformed men are everywhere in New York, but the SWAT units should have been a clue. As soon as Robert realized his was up shit creek, Attila took him down. The police assumed he had a detonator on him. Robert didn't know what hit him and he was in handcuffs before he had a chance to blink. The bomb squad was there and got the bomb. I later found out it had a manual timer.

Somehow Robert got the impression the K-9 officer would have trouble controlling the dog. Unless Robert was very frank about the location of his accomplices, Robert might not go to trial with a face.

Twenty minutes later the NYPD arrested Eldon, Eileen and Fenton in a Times Square hotel. Eldon immediately tried to shift the blame to Eileen. Eileen took that badly. The only problem confronting the police was selecting the most probable confession. I was completely in the dark as to what the Police found. This was a NYPD collar, and there were delicate negotiations between the Richmond Police and the NYPD and to who would get to prosecute whom for what. I would have to wait.

The Duke of Richmond Players production of Shakespeare's Midsummer's Night Dream went on as scheduled. One of the Times' theater reviewers dropped in to take a quick look and stayed for the entire play. The review the next morning was, "Brilliant, clever, bawdy and rolling-in-the-aisles funny."

We were to have had a seven performance run, but they added a Sunday performance and three matinees. The sponsoring foundation looked good; the Duke of Richmond Players was covered in glory and the actors, designers and crewmembers had a resume item that was hard to beat.

The theater is not my life, so the play was just an interesting experience for me. It would have been more fun without three dead bodies and a concussion, but it was fun. It was a life changing experience for Charlie and Skyler who were now much in demand. They stayed with the Duke of Richmond's Company but had numerous commissions for other work.

Frederic's career came to life again. He no longer had to play Santa at Christmas. The little people s' careers took off too. Rudolph told me they were still a novelty acts, but they had proved they could act.

Saul came to Richmond two weeks later to sort things out with Dean. Dean had been out of the loop to since the New York District Attorney negotiated with the Richmond Commonwealth's Attorney. There would be no trials, only sentencing. The confessions made trials unnecessary.

The whole chain of events started with the ill-fated production of Hamlet. It was just a series of nasty pranks that got out of hand. Eldon Jones' personality was at the core of the problem. His ego was double the size of his abilities. He was never wrong and not capable of admitting anything wrong. His ego required unwavering admiration and hero worship.

Eldon was an impressive and attractive man in many ways and he attracted followers. A normal person, such as Rufus, would soon realize Eldon's abilities didn't justify the worship. However, a small group never wavered. Many of them suffered from the same delusional visions as Eldon. He told them they were undiscovered talents with great gifts, neglected by a world filled with no talent peons.

Eldon believed in natural genius and told his followers their talents were such, that study, educations and hard work were unnecessary.

Anyone who didn't recognize these talents were fool, and dangerous fool who held the genius back from his or her potential.

Apparently Eldon despised Charlie and hated the success of Queen Macbeth . He must have noticed Midsummer was going to be another success. Eileen was involved in the earlier poison pen event and suggested that as a way to through things off kilter in the play. Eldon knew Fenton and had been trying to help him.

Skyler's partner Maurice heard Robert calling in to Eileen with information for the next nasty letter. As Skyler surmised Maurice confronted Robert; there was a scuffle, and Maurice fell, fracturing his skull and dying. It was manslaughter at the most.

I recognized Robert was an ass-hole, but I hadn't realized just how bad his was. He didn't like Maurice, so killing him didn't bother him much. It really bothered Eldon. Eldon had hopes that he would find an academic position at a major university. If anyone found out about the poison pen letters, Eldon was toast. The death made it much more likely the source of the letters would be found. Eldon knew the police were on the site, but not that I was working on it too.

Complicating the matter was the lack of command and control. Robert, Eileen, Emma and Fenton essentially were independent contractors. Eldon suggested they might do something. He didn't tell them what to do, and he was careful to maintain deniability. Emma's bomb was a total shock to him.

Eldon knew Fenton and knew about Fenton's problem with sexual aggression, i.e. rape. It is a mark of Eldon's stunning over confidence, that he counseled Fenton himself rather than turning Fenton over to a professional counselor or the police. Elton believed most of Fenton's stories were fantasies. Fenton told him he never actually made sexual contact with his prey. He neglected to tell Fenton that he had a problem with premature ejaculation, and there was DNA evidence.

Saul wasn't impressed by Elton telling him that while he knew Fenton was assaulting women. Apparently, that was acceptable since Fenton didn't rape or kill his victims. "Eldon Jones is a rare piece of work," Saul remarked.

"Who killed Emma?" I asked.

"Eileen did her in. The bombing was more unexpected by Eldon than by her. He had no idea. Eileen had been in on the bomb plot but never thought Emma would go through with it. Eldon was enraged; Eileen denied any knowledge of it and then went to see Emma. They knew they were in deep trouble," Saul said, "Did you know Emma?"

"I met her," I replied. "She was a classic weak link. She didn't know enough to know what she didn't know. Who killed Milton?"

"That was Elton himself," Saul replied, "Milton guessed who was behind the problems. He had a brief fling with Robert. Apparently, he like young men, and Robert was young enough. Milton discovered Robert was not his type and he was defiantly not his type. Robert was straight. "Robert dropped by once and a while and let something drop."

"Milton realized something was up and called Elton. My guess is Milton knew something was up, but not the full extent of the problems. He thought the deaths were accidental." Elton wasn't technically guilty of anything, but Milton said he would spill the beans to Dean. A scandal like that would spread like wildfire through the groves of academe. Elton's chance to get a position in a college ever again would have been doomed. That sealed Milton's doom."

"Eileen's interest in early anarchism was at the root of the varied crimes involved," Saul explained. "Anarchists didn't believe in organization. A leader might say attack a world leader, but the persons and techniques were left up to their followers. There was no central direction, only inspiration."

"Thus we had a poison pen letter, a bombing, rape and an accident?"

"That's right, Clydesdale," Saul said.

"Charley called me a few days ago and asked if I'd like to play the gravedigger in Hamlet," I said. "I think I will stick to detecting. It seems to be safer."

# About the Author

Bob Archman is a retired man living in rural Virginia. He has liked mysteries ever since he got his first Hardy Boy's book in 1957. He also likes Agatha Christie's mature detectives, Hercule Poirot and Jane Marple. He is interested in relationships between mature, hard working men. He tends to write about men who are actively engaged in their jobs and life and happen to be gay, rather than gay men who happen to have a job. A friend of his once asked, "Why be gay and not like sex?" Most of the men in Bob Archman's novels know the answer to that question.

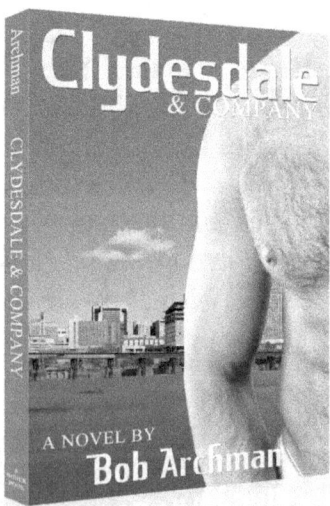

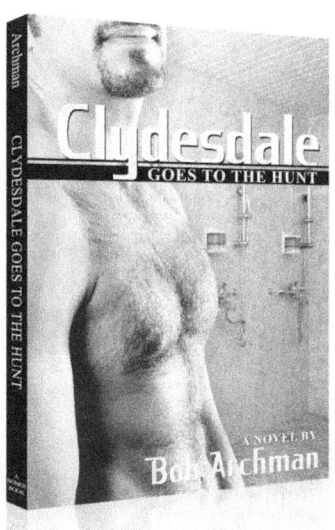

Archman

**Clydesdale**
**GOES TO THE HUNT**

CLYDESDALE GOES TO THE HUNT

A NOVEL BY
**Bob Archman**

Archman

**Clydesdale**
GOES TO A FUNERAL

CLYDESDALE GOES TO A FUNERAL

A NOVEL BY
**Bob Archman**

Archman

**Clydesdale**
GOES TO WASHINGTON

CLYDESDALE GOES TO WASHINGTON

A NOVEL BY
**Bob Archman**

Archman

**Clydesdale**
MOVES TO ESSEX PARK

DESDALE MOVES ESSEX PARK

A NOVEL BY
**Bob Archman**

www.ingramcontent.com/pod-product-compliance
Lightning Source LLC
Chambersburg PA
CBHW051145260626
47170CB00005B/1963